A CAGE OF CURSED SOULS

A DARK AND TWISTED TALES

NOVELLA

ISBN 978-1-960411-99-0

Published by Night Muse Press

Cover Art by Maria Spada

Character Art by Kalynne Art

Editing by Nastasia Bishop in collaboration with Stardust Book Services

Formatted by R. L. Davennor

CONTENT WARNING

This novella contains graphic depictions of violence and death and adult language. It is intended for a mature adult audience.

To those who fight against the evils of the world.

1. BOUNTIES & BLADES

That word was sour on my tongue as I sat perched on a rooftop overlooking the docks. The setting sun dipped below the horizon casting the port in darkness, save for the lanterns that hung on various posts. Most of the sailors found themselves already tucked away in the few inns Chione had to offer. All except for one. A man whose name evaded me. His tricorn hat covered most of his face, but his crimson waistcoat bore a sigil I hadn't seen in the Enchanted Realm in a very long time.

Kingsman.

Though he wasn't who I waited for. He stood near his ship speaking to a stout man with curly black hair and two swords draped along his back. They were just out of earshot, and it was too dark to read their lips, but I didn't need to see to know why they were here. The Queen of the Enchanted Realm and the King of Khan were in the process of an alliance. A truce that would finally bring our two kingdoms together.

I scanned the docks for the hooded figure. Still nothing, but with the kingsman in sight, it wouldn't take long for the vigilante to show up. It had taken me three days of scouring the damn city to track down her next target. I hadn't any idea what she wanted with a kingsman, but I'd find out soon enough.

The Hoods always got their targets. My brothers and I lived by a code, by the rules and laws governed by a righteous and strong queen. Whereas this masked foe preyed on anyone they deemed a threat with no regard for anyone else or the law.

A shadow on the other side of the docks caught my attention. No, not a shadow.

The Masked Maiden.

Vigilante of Chione.

Lawbreaker.

My target.

She stepped out into the soft glow of the moon. The thick cloak and hood she wore confirmed her identity. Even shadowed beneath the cowl of material, I could see the toned skin underneath—save for the eyes and nose which were always covered by a mask. She stayed on the other side of the docks, frozen as her gaze fell on the captain.

I stepped down from the roof and shimmied down a drainpipe, feet silent as they reached the cobblestone, and I kept between the buildings, out of sight. I'd been built around stealth, my body melting into shadows and puffs of smoke in a blink of an eye—a gift given to me by my fae mother.

Which made me one of the best assassins in the Brotherhood. The ability to not only dissolve into shadows but to also shift into a cloud of smoke or change my appearance completely—though the latter only worked for short periods of time. All of this made me the queen's greatest asset.

As I peered around the building, the Masked Maiden had already started advancing toward the captain and his cohort. Moving from one cover to another, she looked like a lioness. Light on her feet, she didn't stalk or stomp but glided with a grace that reminded me of the Hoods. I found myself entranced by her movements, so much so that I nearly forgot why I was out here in the first place.

Leaving the confines of the shadows, I knelt next to a set of wine barrels and sucked in a deep breath. My lungs filled with crisp night air as magic coursed through my veins. Wisps of black smoke billowed at my feet. It curled around my ankles, up and over my shoulders, until nothing but darkness remained.

My body morphed between one breath and the next, leaving behind my human form for dark, thick, smog. While people could see this form, they'd never know who was beneath it—something the queen found useful.

I weaved around boxes and barrels along the port's main street, glancing over obstacles until she came into view. Only a few feet in front of me now as she slithered closer. Her mask may have covered her face, but I still sensed the readiness in her. The desire to slide whatever blade she wielded into the heart of the captain behind me.

I'd strike her down before she ever got the chance.

As she moved around the final barrier that kept us apart, I sprung and coalesced from the smoke, back to the assassin for a brief second. I knocked into her and the black smoke that clung to me swallowed us whole.

"What the fuck!" she yelled.

I dipped into my senses, and let my magic do its work. Not fear or dread, but raw anger so potent it pulsed right along with her racing heart. Her raw emotion consumed me

She writhed beneath me as she kicked and screamed in an attempt to get away. But she couldn't. Not while wrapped in my magic, anyway.

We drifted through the streets, maneuvering around buildings and alleyways until we reached the opposite end of Chione, then I let go, letting her fall into a bale of hay next to the stables.

My smoke dissipated, leaving the human behind, and the Maiden shrieked.

"What the fuck are you?" she spat and rolled to her feet.

"You sure like that word, don't you?" I said.

"I prefer my dagger in your chest much better."

I ducked just in time as a knife whirled past my head. "You may need to work on your ... *oof.*"

She leapt on top of me, and we crumbled to the ground. Her fists pummeled me left and right as I held mine up to protect me. With all my strength, I pushed my hips upward and rolled, sending both of us twirling until I straddled over her. She bucked and kicked and managed to land a scratch along my face, but I refused to let up. I grabbed her wrists and slammed them above her, only then had I noticed that her hood had fallen.

Dark ebony hair sat in a puddle around her head. Her complexion, much darker than I'd originally thought, shoned against the moon's glow. Bright red eyes scowled beneath a black mask trimmed in lace that curved around her cheek bones. She blinked once, then twice, before warm brown replaced the red.

What the…

"Stop. Fighting." I hissed and gritted my teeth while she continued to flail underneath me. How was she not tired yet?

"Piss off." She spat again, this time getting some in my eye. She bucked once more, taking advantage of the distraction, and got a hand away from me. I made a grab for it, but she twirled around, and a dagger appeared in my vision, one that she pointed to my manhood.

"Get off me, or junior here will never know the inside of a woman again."

"Is that what you told the other men you've slaughtered?" I ground out.

She huffed; her dagger held firm as she crawled out from beneath me. "Those men deserved what they got."

"That's not for you to decide."

Only the queen and the Brotherhood decided who lived and died in the Enchanted Realm. Not some girl who had no regard for life.

"Says who? The Evil Queen?" She threw her head back and

laughed. "She's far worse than any of the men I've killed. I kill because no one else will do it, because corruption and darkness seeps into this realm and no one is doing anything about it."

What the hells was she talking about? Evil Queen. I'd never heard that name before. I'd also never known the queen to be evil in any way. The only evil I knew stood in front of me and I'd find any means to stop her.

"The queen doesn't kill unnecessarily. People must be put on trial, must be given a chance to plead their case before being cut down."

"You assassins are all the same, so wrapped around the fingers of a terrible woman, all you can see is great tits and a pretty face. Tell me, *Hood*, do you even know the people you place your allegiance to? Those Elders who think of themselves as almighty gods?" She snarled and raised her dagger to my chest. "I may be a vigilante for the injustices of this world, but at least I'm not a man who can't even open his eyes to the devil who sits at the head of a table created from lies and deception."

Hot, tangible fury dug into every crevice of my being. How dare she speak about the queen, about the Elders, in such a way? She had no idea what burdens they carried every day, what choices and decisions they had to make for the greater good.

"Enough of this," I said, and took a step closer until my chest pressed up against the dagger. Being an assassin taught me that fear was useless, nothing more than a distraction and a weakness.

Her eyes widened, and her lips parted. I took in every inch of her. The darkness in her eyes, the leather, the weapons that sat in different places along her body. All of her. While I didn't know what to expect when going up against the Masked Maiden, I hadn't expected this. Dark hues of red and black, mixed in a swirl of bright green, bloomed around her. Her aura. An aura said a lot about someone; I'd only touched on the subject as a student, never finding the need to learn more about something as trivial as an aura, and yet I now wished I had taken the time. Losing myself in one's aura didn't happen often, hells it didn't happen at all, yet right now I wanted to devour every inch of it. To soak it in.

I shook my head. *What magic did this woman possess?* It must have been strong. I needed to stand my ground, to remember my mission.

Bring in the threat.

Vigilante.

The Masked Maiden.

I looked down at the dagger in her hand. She may be wielding a weapon, but I had the upper hand. I sucked in a deep breath and let it out as thick smoke swelled between us. "I'm taking you in."

Before I uttered another word, she lowered her dagger and sailed her knee into my groin. I yelped and fell to my knees as pain coursed through me in waves. I bit my tongue to keep from crying out further.

She knelt beside me, turning her dagger over in her hands as she pressed her lips to my ear.

"As fun as this has been, I have things to do and people to … slaughter." She wrinkled her nose as she said that final word.

The Maiden turned to leave, but I grabbed her wrist. "You're not going anywhere. I won't—"

Pain tore through the back of my head, and I cried out. The world spun around me as specks of light danced in my vision. I touched the back of my head, wincing at the pain as I brought my hand back.

Blood.

"See you around, Hood."

I blinked several times, trying to clear my vision but only a silhouette came into view.

She laughed and vanished into the night.

I brought my gelding, Sherwood, to a stop in front of the pub and slid from the saddle. Sunlight warmed my back as I gave him a pat and palmed a handful of oats. Around me, the villagers' stares weighed down my shoulders. After years of being a Brother, of being an assassin, one would think the looks wouldn't bother me anymore. Yet they did, and as conversations turned to whispers, I couldn't help but wonder what secrets they were spreading. Or what monstrous things they spewed.

Sherwood finished his oats, and I wiped my hand on my pants before tying him to a post. My head still pounded from whatever the Maiden hit me with, but at least the bleeding had stopped.

Glancing behind me, a group of young women in fancy, fluffy dresses and large hats hurried inside a bakery. The few children who gaped at me were shooed by their parents back inside the church and the men across the street who worked in the blacksmith's stopped their hammering. Though it was the Masked Maiden they should fear, their eyes pierced through me as if I were the plague of Chione.

Collecting my wits, I left Sherwood and headed into the pub. My nose wrinkled at the stench of vomit and stale alcohol. It nearly stopped me in my tracks, but I pushed through the patrons until I reached the counter. A lanky man with a balding head narrowed his beady eyes at me as he poured a drink. Salt and pepper scruff covered his chin, and his arms were lined with faded ink.

"Robin," he cursed. "What in hell's sake are you doing here? If you so much as break one—"

"There will be no breaking of anything today, Eddard. Any chance you have a second? I need information." I pulled out a coin purse and set it on the sticky counter. Eddard passed me a glass before swiping the purse and peering inside.

His brow rose. "This is a lot of gold."

"Aye, think of it as repayment for the mess I made last time."

Recalling my last visit, I winced as I remembered broken chairs, glasses, and a few faces. When that happened, it usually meant paying out a large sum to whoever owned such items. The civilians of Chione considered me a 'ruthless assassin,' but I was still a man of honor. I replaced broken things, repaid all debts, ensured no child I saw on the streets went hungry, and every day before her passing, I cared for the woman who raised me. A stranger who took me in, an orphan on the streets, and cared for me more than anyone else in the Enchanted Realm ever had.

But no one cared about the good deeds I did because I would always be an assassin. Our reputation of ruthlessness carried throughout the city. Most of the assassin's enjoyed being the boogeymen of Chione— but not me. I hated being looked at as the enemy, hated seeing the disgust in their faces. But nothing would change their minds about me, and I'd learned to deal with it.

"Well then, what do you need?"

There weren't many people in Chione who knew the ins and outs of who came and went in the port, but Eddard had his crows. Homeless children who he used as eyes and ears, reporting back to him for warm food.

"The kingsman who arrived last night. Where is he staying?" With luck, the captain had found his way to one of the inns before the Maiden found her way back to the docks. I needed to find him and ensure his safe passage to the queen. This alliance between Khan and Chione was important to Queen Gemma, which meant it was important to all of us.

"The pirate?" Eddard spat. "He came in here last night right before closing. Him and his damned men nearly drank this pub dry. Had to send the twins to come get him."

Shit. "The Hunter's Inn?"

Eddard nodded. "Now, if you don't have any more questions. I have patrons to serve."

With a wave, the man returned to his pouring, and I stewed on what to do. The twins were the last people I wanted to deal with today. I downed the alcohol and made my way back to Sherwood.

His tail swished back and forth as a small boy in white pet his mane and fed him an apple.

A smile tugged on my lips as I watched. Children were so innocent, a breath of fresh air in a world built on death, war, and treaties. An ache festered in my chest, digging and scraping at an old wound that would never cease. My father had died on the battlefield, and my mother's grief sent her to an early grave. They left me with nothing more than a few coins to my name and Sherwood. He wasn't just a horse, but a member of the fae family. He'd lived nearly two life spans before coming into my father's possession. Him and I had been through a lot together.

"He'll dance for you if you scratch under his ear."

The boy jumped and whirled around. His face melted to a ghostly white as he stuttered. "I-I … I didn't mean … He just—"

"Whoa, kid. It's fine, Sherwood loves the attention. Go ahead, give him a scratch."

"Okay," the boy said. His voice rose in excitement. "I've never seen a horse dance before."

Sherwood, the good boy, lowered his head so the boy could reach. As soon as his hand scratched the horse's favorite spot, his feet marched in place, and he let out a lengthy sigh.

The boy giggled and marched his own feet along with Sherwood. I leaned against a post, watching the two of them as they danced and enjoyed each other's company. I opened my mouth to tell him that we had to go when a shout rang from across the street.

"Logan Charles Summers, what do you think you're doing?" A woman stomped over, her purple skirt bunched up into her hand and her face nearly as red as the apple the boy had fed Sherwood.

"Playing with the horse, Mama."

The woman scowled, flicking her eyes up and down my length as if I were nothing more than one of the drunks who frequented the pub behind me. But that wasn't it. It may have only been a flash, but I saw it: the fear and worry of what I could do. The Queen's Assassin. A man who knows nothing more than his job. It was total bullshit of course, and she—as well as everyone else—would know that if they actually took the time to get to know me.

Before I could utter a word, Logan's mother hauled him away. Tears rolled down his cheeks. He glanced back at me, but I tore my gaze from him and back to Sherwood. It was better this way, for everyone to fear me, to think of me as the monster. It made my job much easier.

A job I needed to get back to.

"Well, boy, time to go see the twins."

11. DANGEROUS CHOICES

THE LAST TWO PEOPLE I WANTED TO SEE TODAY WERE Hansel and Gretel.

Not because I wasn't fond of them—on the contrary, they were some of the best people in Chione—but because they weren't subtle by any means, and I needed that right now.

Silence greeted me as I entered the Inn. The patrons were either still asleep or hadn't started their daily dose of drinking. Hopefully that meant I had time to speak with the twins before prying ears could butt in.

They stood behind a large wooden desk; their backs turned to me as they shifted through papers.

"I told you it was here a second ago," Hansel's voice rumbled.

"Right, just like earlier when my apple pie went mysteriously missing," Gretel snarled back.

Hansel whirled to Gretel, a finger hanging in the air between them. "You're the one who left it sitting on the edge of an open window. Who knows what kind of creatures snatched your pie."

Gretel smacked Hansel's hand away. "No one takes my pie, Hans, no one."

"Good to know you two are still such loving siblings."

The two of them spun around, and smiles spread along their faces. "Hansel, look who it is. Mr. Assassin."

Definitely not subtle.

"I can see that, Gretel. I'm not blind." Hansel rolled his eyes as he jumped over the desk and smacked my shoulders. "Good to see you, mate."

Hansel towered over me. Dark, long braided hair fell over broad shoulders and his black shirt and breeches made his skin appear as white as the sandy beaches of Nonoke Island. He smelled of mint, pine, and possibly a hint of apples.

"You too." I nodded behind him. "Gretel."

"What brings you to our humble abode?"

Gretel spread her hands out over the desk and leaned into it. Lace fabric traced along her arms and ended at her shoulders where the rest of the shirt exposed her neck and cleavage. Dark brown hair was pulled up into a tight bun, from which something stuck out. I stifled my grin. Leave it to Gretel to have a knife holding her hair in place. No doubt there were several more hidden beneath her bodice, even more strapped to her legs—I'd had a personal relationship with the one strapped to her boot. I ran a finger along the base of my neck, a mark long since healed and scarred.

"I'm hoping you two can help me with a little problem."

They froze. Understanding lit their faces and they wasted no time in dragging me away from the front of the Inn to somewhere more private.

I'd called on the twins' services a few times during my assignments; witches always came in handy when dealing with difficult law breakers. Their abilities weren't always clear to me, but Gretel had a knack for healing and Hansel had one hells of a sleight of hand. Though most of the time their help had more to do with distractions, including, but not limited to, "blowing shit up," as Hansel would say.

All they'd ever asked for in return were chocolates from the queen's personal stash, brought in from Khan and sold only to the royal family. And every once in a while they'd ask for something a little more personal. I didn't have time for such pleasures today, unfortunately.

"Who are we blowing up?" Hansel grinned and rubbed his hands together.

"No blowing off limbs needed today. What I do need is to know what room the kingsman is staying in and if the room next to him is available?"

"The kingsman?" Gretel asked.

"The drunken sod you picked up from Eddard's pub."

"Ah, that guy, yeah he's upstairs in room 4." Gretel narrowed her eyes. "Is this a royal thing?"

In other words, had I planned to assassinate a man inside the Inn. I knew the rules; troubles were fine to bring into the Inn, but anything involving death had to be done outside the establishment. Cleaning up a little blood here and there didn't attract too much attention but having to haul out a body tended to send the wrong message. The twins worked hard to keep this place a sanctuary for lost souls. A place that welcomed everyone no matter what side of the gates they lived on.

"It is, but I'm only here to escort the kingsman to the queen in one piece."

There would be no killing today. Not unless the Maiden came waltzing about and decided to try something stupid.

Gretel nodded. "Good, I can have room 5 available in a few minutes. Help yourself to some pie while you wait." Gretel shot Hansel a look. "Oh, I'm sorry, I forgot my brother's a damn pig and ate it."

I sighed and left the two of them to their childish bickering. I really could have gone for some apple pie too, but I had a kingsman to introduce myself to. Were the rest of his crew lurking about, or did they stay on the ship? It wouldn't have been wise for the man to walk the streets without protection. I'm sure he had enough people to help escort him to the castle, but they didn't know Chione as I did, and with the Maiden around, I wasn't going to chance it. He and his crew were just going to have to deal with an additional member on their journey to the castle.

The floorboards creaked under my weight as I made my way to the second floor. Lanterns lit on either side of the walls illuminated the way forward. I stopped when my gaze met two men standing guard at a door. Their stares dug into me, assessing a possible threat to their captain.

The guard closest to me hovered a twitching hand over the weapon on his hip and the other pushed himself off the wall he'd been leaning against.

"Can we help you?"

"A word with your captain would be sufficient. I'm from the queen's guard."

They eyed me, taking in the hood over my head, the dagger on my hip, and the lack of armor along my frame. No one who saw me would believe me to be just a guard of the queen, but they didn't need to. I would get in that room one way or another.

Twitchy-hand lifted his chin. "Captain Adrian has made it clear no one is to disturb him until he says otherwise. I'm afraid you'll have to wait."

"All right, then you'll be just fine when the king asks why your captain is dead and the person who did it isn't apprehended."

The other guard took a step closer. "Is that a threat?"

"You can take that statement however you please, it doesn't change the fact that someone is out to kill him and if you don't let me speak to him, you'll both be answering to King Roland." I let a grin show on my face and dropped my voice to a whisper. "Isn't he the one with the notorious guillotine?"

Both guards went pale at my words and hastily turned to knock on the door. Curses, crashes, and grumbling rose from the room before the door flung open. The captain on the other side wore nothing more than a long undershirt and long black socks. His eyes, bloodshot and an odd shade of green, flickered from his guards to me.

"What is the meaning of this?" His gravelly, deep voice exposed just how much alcohol he'd consumed the night prior.

"Apologies, Captain, this man tells us there's a threat on your life.

Apparently, he's one of Queen Gemma's guards."

Captain Adrian sighed and rubbed a hand along his face. "If I had a coin for every time someone threatened my life, I'd be richer than the damn queen herself. As you can see, I have guards posted at my door. No threat will get to me so long as my men hold their ground. Now go away, and let me sleep for sea's sake."

The door slammed, and his guards moved in front to block it. Fine. The captain may not have realized the danger, but I did, and I refused to let this man die for his stupidity. I nodded to the guards and walked down the hall until I stopped at my room.

"What do you think you're doing?" twitchy-hand guard asked.

"Well, you see this place here is called an Inn. It's where people come to sleep and get drunk and have sexual relations in secret." I winked before opening the door and stepping inside.

A small bed sat on one side of the room, and a desk with a dresser made of dark mahogany wood sat on the other side. Blue, lace curtains were drawn over the window but light still seeped through. I unbuttoned my cloak and laid it over the desk chair before sitting on the bed. I'd sit here until either the captain sobered up enough to head to the castle, or the Maiden showed up.

Either way, I'd be ready.

Captain Adrian slept through the day. For a man who traveled with pirates, he hadn't handled his liquor very well.

I stood from the bed and made my way to the window. After opening the curtains, and then the window, I peered outside to see a pitch-black sky riddled with specks of light. From this point in town, I could make out just about all the main business. Candles flickered in windows, smoke billowed from chimneys, and children's laughter in the distance had my shoulders relaxing. I leaned against the windowsill. Cool night air curled around my warm skin sending gooseflesh down my arms. Only food and company would make this night any better.

Gretel slept only a few doors down from here. I had to keep my focus on the drunken captain, otherwise I'd have already knocked on her door. The pretty Maiden with eyes sharper than the dagger at my hip flooded into my mind, and I squeezed my eyes shut and shook my head. Closing my eyes only made seeing her worse. The way her bodice curved right along with her frame, or the way amusement had flashed in her eyes when she'd said she'd see me around. Something about her seemed so familiar. She was a wanted woman. A criminal with no regard for the law. She had to be stopped, and one way or another, I'd make it happen.

Something pricked at the back of my neck, and I searched the ground for any signs of movement. Nothing out of the ordinary, yet something still felt off.

Better go check on the captain.

After buttoning my cloak, I tossed the hood over my head and made my way down the hall.

This time, a set of different guards stood against the door. Shift change.

"You're not permitted entry. Captain has made it clear that he is to not be disturbed, even by a man in a hood who thinks there's someone after him. However, he doesn't want to offend the queen, so he has agreed to let you accompany us to the castle."

Let me? I wanted to slap my knee and keel over in a fit of laughter. Did he really think he had a choice?

"Have you checked on him recently?" I asked. The bad feeling reached the pit of my stomach.

"That's hardly any of your—"

A crashing noise sounded from the room. This time there were no grunts or curses, nothing but utter silence.

Shit.

"You need to get in there right now," I said.

Before he could speak, a stifled scream sent me bursting into the room, ignoring the two men who didn't even have a second to react.

I only had a moment to take in the room.

Captain Adrian laid sprawled out on the bed, a sock stuffed into his mouth and his limbs tied to the corners of the bed frame. Blood coated the white linens and I winced. Gretel was going to be pissed. Small cuts covered the captain's chest. How in sea's sake had I not heard this? Standing over him with a knife drawn stood the Maiden. Her hood laid behind her exposing a long dark braid that reached the middle of her back. Hues of red pulsed around her in a nearly blinding light.

"What the hells is going on here?" One of the guards gasped behind me. "Captain?"

The Maiden whirled toward me.

"You," she snarled. "Get the fuck out. This doesn't concern you."

"Put down the weapon and all of us can walk away with"—I peered down at Adrian—"most of our dignity."

"Dignity?" The Maiden threw her head back and laughed. "You think this man deserves that? Do you even know what he has on his ship right now? What *gift* he has for your precious queen?"

She took a step forward, her blade inched to the man's throat.

"He's from Khan; I expect he has several different gifts."

"Oh, don't act like you don't know. Her precious *assassin*."

She said that word with such distaste, as if it pained her to say it. I'd been doing this job for a few years now, and the people never changed. Their views never changed. They rushed off to hide, and those brave enough, those who considered us nothing more than scum of the realm, simply stared us down. I spent every day protecting this place, sacrificing everything to bring peace and honor to Chione. I wasn't always privy to what went on during a council meeting. The queen and the Elders worried about those things. According to them, assassins only needed to enforce the laws, not be there while they're being made.

"The kingsman is here to negotiate an alliance. He's not—"

"He's a damn flesh trader. It's their main purpose. You don't know the type of people that come into your port?" She clicked her tongue. "And here I thought you assassins knew everything. Pity."

Adrian tried to speak, his voice muffled by the sock, and to my surprise the Maiden plucked it from his mouth. He gagged before clearing his throat. "If you let me go, I could make you very—"

"I don't want your money or anything else you have to offer." The

Maiden lifted the dagger and turned toward me. "But it appears I won't get what I want while the assassin is here."

"How about you drop the knife, and you can tell me all about what it is you want." I took several steps, each one deliberate and calculated. If I got close enough to the bed maybe I'd be able to lunge and stop her before the bloody blade did any more damage.

Sparks of red danced in her eyes as she focused them on me. A flash of realization came and went on her face.

"How close are you to her?"

"Excuse me?"

The Maiden rolled her eyes. "The queen, are you a personal assassin of hers? Does she know your name? Do you know her itinerary?"

"I don't see how this is relevant."

The captain tugged against his restraints. "It seems the two of you have a lot to talk about. If one of you wouldn't mind just cutting me loose—"

"Bite your tongue, flesh trader. You're not going anywhere," the Maiden said, without looking away from me. "Just answer the question already."

"Why would I do that?"

"If you answer, I promise not to kill the kingsman."

Promise? As if I'd trust her to keep her word. She obviously came here to kill him. What did that have to do with me? Maybe she decided to concoct an elaborate scheme to… to what exactly? Distract me? Gain leverage on the queen? The latter seemed unlikely given the questions she asked. I needed to be smart here.

"The queen knows all her assassins. By name and rank. It's good to know who works for you."

"So, you know all about the underground pits? You're okay with the illegal activities that go on down there?"

What?

Queen Gemma had ensured all illegal activities were demolished upon her rule. The streets were clean, the prisons were mostly empty, and I hadn't had to kill anyone in a very long time—a few brawls and the need to put people in their place. The Brotherhood knew everything that went on in the city. But what would the Maiden gain from telling me this? Another distraction, perhaps?

I needed to end this. Her reasons for torturing a man didn't matter to me. She could spout all her deeds to the Council of Elders.

"I think there's been enough talk for one night. Drop the blade or I'll make you."

Before I could even flinch, the Maiden darted forward, but I moved much faster. I called upon the smoke and leapt over the bed, tackling her as we crashed into the side table and pieces of wooden shrapnel sprayed against the wall.

Gretel's really going to kill me.

Shoving that aside, I let go of the smoke and held the Maiden down. Now that I knew the strength it took to keep her still, I held her in place. She must have used all her energy torturing the captain because she barely bucked underneath me.

"Captain?" The guards rushed to Adrian's side.

"Get him untied and take him to room 7. Gretel will know what to do," I said, never taking my eyes from the Maiden. "She'll see to it that the captain arrives at the castle unharmed."

The guards gathered the captain and rushed out of the room and down the hall.

The Maiden squirmed under my hold.

"Stop that," I hissed and stood, bringing her along with me.

"I will once you let me go."

"Not a chance," I bit out. With my hands wrapped around her wrists, I closed my eyes for the briefest of moments and let the magic coursing through my veins do its work. Dark swirls of smoke wrapped around the Maiden's wrists keeping her bound and in place.

"What the hell?" She tried to free her hands, but the magic shackle held firm.

We needed to head to the castle, but with the captain in such terrible shape, leaving now would be dangerous and stupid. Thankfully, Gretel had a little magic of her own and with luck we'd be on the way to the queen by morning.

"Just a little binding magic, shouldn't hurt much. Now, shall we start with the real reason you maimed a captain?"

The Maiden laughed. "Piss off, I don't have to tell you a damn thing. Especially not to a pet of the Bitch Queen."

Anger filtered through the cracks of my guise, though not enough for her to notice. I sucked in a breath and kept my face as neutral as possible.

"You probably should reconsider. You're a wanted woman, a criminal who must face the damage you've created. Think of me as your defense, as the only person in this realm who may be able to save you."

She shot me a look, one of deep hatred and loathing. "Save me? No one can fucking save me. Trust me I've tried to …"

"Oh, don't stop now, we were just getting started," I said, throwing a bit more of my fae charm her way. She struggled against it, against the desire to spill everything, to tell me exactly about her mission and any possible allies she may have. I pulled a bit harder, dug a little deeper, and yet she still relented.

Strong.

Did she have fae lineage in her family? It very well could be possible. It took more strength than most had to combat such magic— magic that I'd been honing for years. Yet somehow she'd managed to keep her mouth shut. To resist me. I curled my hands into fists at my side as I drew on more magic than should have been necessary.

The Maiden let out a breathless snarl. "You *bastard*. I … I have to save them all. F-free them. Stop them from … from …" She cursed again before her shoulders sagged.

Save who?

Stop what?

The illegal activities she went on about, or something else? There were too many questions and even more uncertainty settling in my stomach. My fae charm had the ability to pull words from unwilling participants, but I always had a hard time deciphering truth from lies.

The queen had to know about illegal activities, wouldn't she? For years she demanded order in Chione. She'd worked hard to create a well-oiled machine that had been under her rule for years ever since the king's death nearly half a decade ago. She'd taken the Enchanted Realm from poverty to riches in a matter of months, and at its center, Chione had thrived. Nowhere else in the world had a place been more alive. Whatever misguided thoughts the Maiden had, the queen had no part in it.

Still. Something about her words, about the desperation in her tone, had me faltering for a moment.

"What kind of things do you think the queen allows?" I asked, once again pulling on my charm.

"Stop doing that!" she hissed. "I can talk about truths without your damned magic, Hood."

I let my charm falter, and she sucked in a deep breath. Her chest rose and fell, though her eyes still held their ground, staring at me with an overwhelming sense of intensity.

"So then tell me what activities you think are going on. What do you think the queen is doing, the same queen who has demanded order since the moment the Elder's placed the crown upon her head."

She paused for a moment, probably considering what to tell me. Not that it mattered, if she didn't want to tell me, I'd simply use my charm to get it out of her. One way or another I'd get answers.

"It would be much better if I could show you, but you'll need to take this off first." She raised her arms and nodded to the cuffs.

"Right, and then the second those come off you'll have your dagger on my throat before I can blink. I don't think so."

The Maiden let out a frustrated sigh. "Look, I've got nothing left to lose, but there are others who are suffering. It's not about trust, it's not about who has the upper hand, it's about doing what's right. I can see it in your eyes. You don't want to believe me, but a part of you is curious. So, take these off and let me show you just what it is the queen has done."

This was a bad idea. Horrible, really, but curiosity had me in its grip. I'd been an assassin for the queen for a long time, but I also served the people, a man who simply wanted peace for those who deserved it. If the Maiden spoke the truth, I'd be the one to put an end to it. Whether the queen knew about it or not. I may work for the queen, but my duty to protect and serve the people far outweighed anything else.

"How about a bargain?" I asked.

"What?"

"If you haven't guessed yet, I'm fae, and a fae bargain is one that can't be broken. Think of it as a way to ensure we both keep our word."

She hesitated, considering me for a moment before speaking. "What do you have in mind exactly?"

"Well, I want what's best for the people, and if you say they're suffering, then I want to do something about it."

Her brows rose in what could be taken as surprise.

"The queen may have given me this position, and I may be loyal to the throne, but I'm more loyal to the people of this city. No matter what you may think of me. So, you have the rest of the night to convince me of your accusations, and if you do, I'll help you free whoever it is that needs to be freed. No harm will come to you during this bargain, but if you fail to convince me by the time the sun rises, you will come with me and pay for the deaths and chaos you've caused. No harm will come to me either during this bargain."

We remained silent for so long, I wasn't sure she'd ever answer. Had

I done something stupid and rash? By her silence, I figured this was all a very bad idea. Yet, what harm could be done with such a bargain?

Finally, she said, "All right, we have a deal, but I want one other thing added to this bargain."

"Go on."

"When you find out the truth about the queen and what's going on right under your nose, I want an apology."

"An apology?"

"Yes, and it better be a good one."

I laughed. "Deal."

III. ARENA OF BEASTS

SECONDS AFTER THE MAIDEN TOUCHED MY HAND everything went … dull and … dark. As though strings dipped in blackened ink curled themselves around my skin, coating me in a pool of darkness. Hollow and raw.

My smoke had always been airy and light, whatever crawled over my skin now left behind something far darker, and I wanted to jump into a bath and scrub my skin until it left. Though, the minute she let go, it all vanished.

I swallowed the urge to snatch my hand back and step away from her. I'd made bargains with witches, pirates, and even a nymph, but none of them felt as though the seven hells themselves were consuming me.

Never in my life had I felt such darkness, such *suffering*.

Until her.

Whoever did that to her, whoever caused all the anguish building inside her, deserved an assassin's wrath.

Could this be why her aura beamed with a dark red? Why flames seemed to constantly flicker in her eyes? I wanted to ask her. To demand she tell me whatever haunted her.

Instead, I asked, "Where exactly is this underground pit?"

"That's it? That's all it takes for a bargain made with a fae?"

Fae bargains were tricky. Not just the words, but the intent. Either party had to be certain in what they wanted, in the agreement they were making. I didn't need an unbreakable vow, or a gemstone to make a bargain. The second our hands wrapped around the other's wrist, once the words were spoken, my magic tied itself to her and her to me. Usually, the bargain had some sort of effect on the hosts. While I'd felt Death itself consuming me, she appeared just fine. She should have felt something too.

Curious.

"Yes, that's it. Where is this pit?"

The Maiden's gaze hardened before she said, "Lower district."

The lower district? I hadn't been there in several months. They'd had little to no activity, no criminals to capture or people to keep in order. It had been quiet and peaceful.

Had that been the first clue I missed that something was amiss?

"Lead the way." I gestured toward the door.

She opened it just as Gretel appeared on the other side.

Gretel looked at me and then the Maiden before placing her hands on her hips and scowled. "What the hells do you think you're doing,

Hood? I told you… is that a broken table? Is that *blood* on my linens? What in seven seas, Robin?"

I winced. "Sorry, Gretel. I promise as soon as my business is finished, I'll make it up to you."

Before she scolded me some more, I kissed her cheek and ushered the Maiden down the hall and away from the scary woman with far too many pointy objects at her disposal.

Sherwood stood waiting for us as we emerged into the night. He gave the Maiden a wary stare until he saw me. He let out a neigh that I could only interpret as annoyance at being disturbed at such a late hour. We traveled during the night before, but most of the time my night travel involved flinging myself from one rooftop to the other. I gave him a pat and a good scratch and climbed on.

"What are you doing?" The Maiden's eyes widened. "I'm not getting on that damn thing."

Sherwood neighed unhappily and stomped his feet.

"Sherwood doesn't think too highly of you either."

She crossed her arms over her chest and raised a brow. "Still doesn't mean I'm getting on it."

"Is the fierce Masked Maiden afraid of a horse?" I quipped.

"First of all, I'm scared of nothing, and second, don't call me the Masked Maiden or any other stupid false name."

Huh. So, she didn't enjoy the nicknames whispered through Chione. Go figure, neither did I.

I held out my hand. "Then what should I call you?"

She stared at my hand. Unmoving, I waited for her to make a move or to realize that the bargain we made ensured her safety. Sherwood was a good gelding, and while he didn't seem too fond of the Maiden, he'd get us to where we needed to go.

After minutes of staring, she groaned and grabbed my hand, albeit reluctantly, and I hoisted her up. She wrapped her arms around me, clutching my mid-section for dear life.

Finally, she replied, "Marian is fine."

We traveled for a while in silence, save for the click of Sherwood's hooves on the cobblestone. Marian's white-knuckled grip loosened as we trotted on.

We'd have to pass the rest of the districts to get there. Thankfully, the city remained quiet, and while I knew the brotherhood would be out there roaming the streets, I knew their routes and how to evade them. It would have been faster to travel by smoke, but I needed more time to come up with a solid plan. Like what would I do with the information if Marian's claims turned out to be true. No matter what happened, I had to keep my guard up. At least with Sherwood we'd know when someone approached. His ears detected sounds from yards away.

I hoped this was all a distraction, and by morning we'd be headed to the castle.

"There's something you should know before we get there."

I nearly jumped at her words; she'd been so quiet I hadn't expected her to say anything until we got there. Small talk didn't seem to be her thing.

"All right."

"The people there, the ones in charge… they know me and if they see me, if they even catch sight of us, it's all over." I turned and caught a glimpse of fear in her eyes.

"How do they know you exactly?"

She shook her head. "Let's just say I worked for them. I quit, and they didn't approve. But that's not important. I can't go in with you. I-I won't."

What was so terrible about a place that even the Vigilante of Chione refused to enter?

"Don't worry about being seen or noticed."

"Hood, you don't understand, I—"

"It's Robin." I interrupted. My heart hammered in my chest all of a sudden.

"Wh-What?"

"You gave me your name; I only find it fitting that you know mine."

"Well, Robin." Her voice shook ever so slightly. "I don't care what you say. Bargain or not, I agreed to take you, not accompany you inside."

I may be working with her for the time being, but it didn't mean I trusted her. No way in hells would I leave her outside. A part of me wanted to believe the tremble in her voice, but she hadn't given me a reason to yet. And with me, she didn't need to worry about anyone recognizing her. Not when hiding one's identity was a skillset of mine.

"No one will know who you are."

"Hoo ... Robin ... I'm telling you—"

"My smoke will mask your identity. All you have to do is keep your arm linked in mine, and so long as you stick with me, no one will be able to recognize either of us."

Thoughts of Marian's arm linked in mine flooded into my mind's eye. My mouth grew dry, and my stomach curled. It had been a long time since

I'd had a beautiful woman on my arm. A different time and place, I suppose.

"That's … creepy."

I threw my head back and laughed. "I've heard my gift called many things, but creepy has never been one."

"How does it work?" she asked.

"I … I don't really know exactly. I just close my eyes, take a deep breath, and focus on what I want the magic to do. It's limited as all magic is, but it will do the job."

I felt her sit up a little straighter. My heart skipped as her hands moved to rest on my sides. "You've done this before?"

Clearing my throat, I said, "Once or twice."

Or a few hundred.

"All I have to do is touch you and you can make me look different … no one will recognize me?"

"We have to be linked by arms or hands, it doesn't matter, but our limbs must be crossing, but yes that's the gist of it."

It would also wear me down a bit. Under normal circumstances, I changed appearances with painless ease, but having Marian with me would take a bit of my strength. But we weren't going there to cause problems. We'd scope the place out and go back later with a plan.

If there was anything to Marian's words anyway.

"I don't know."

Perhaps a show would help. I gave Sherwood a little tug and he came to a stop.

"What are you doing? We're not there yet."

"A demonstration." I offered her my hand once again, and she took it with less hesitation this time and jumped down from Sherwood.

I pulled her closer until we were a foot apart and watched as her eyes trailed to our linked hands. My chest warmed at her touch, yet for a brief moment that feeling of darkness, of dread and evil, flooded through my mind's eye. What in hells was that? I gave that thought a mental shake and focused on my demonstration.

A never-ending mist swept between us, curving and curling around arms and legs until it swallowed us whole. Marian's eyes widened as they trailed me from head to toe. I knew what she saw; the change of my blonde hair to a dark crimson and eyes nearly as dark as her own. The way my nose grew crooked rather than its normal straight and narrow. I turned her until she faced the window of a closed shop, and her hand flew to her mouth.

Marian's skin lightened to a soft bronze, and her eyes shifted from their normal brown to a light green. She ran an unoccupied hand through her now short hair and giggled. A soft, joyful laugh on the verge of sweetness. A smile crept to my lips.

"This is …" She shook her head. "Exceptionally wild."

Just like her.

I let go of her hand, and in seconds the ruse dissipated.

"I'll take that as a compliment. I promise as long as we stick together everything will be fine. Just keep your arm linked in mine. Are we good?"

Marian turned from the window and nodded swiftly. "Let's do this."

Marian's arm wrapped around my own. Her hood lowered revealing a look of displeasure and unease. She didn't know that I'd done this so many times for the queen. Shifting to appear as a lonely merchant while spying on men who were smuggling illegal goods into port. Or the time I'd shifted to appear as a pirate looking for work when Blackbeard had arrived without warning. Each façad was expertly thought out with a detailed background, and each time I'd done my job successfully. Why should this time be any different?

We rode through the lower district until stopping in front of a building with a sign that read "'Flowers'."

I froze. Bahir's shop. A man who dedicated his life to—as he called it—"saving the world one plant at a time." I had a hard time believing he'd allow illegal activities going on in his shop. Unless he didn't have a choice. It did seem odd that lights shimmered through the windows at such a late hour.

"Are you sure this is the right place?"

"No, I purposefully took you to the wrong side of town," she deadpanned. "And here I thought Queen Gemma's assassins were all smart."

Ignoring her rolling eyes, I opened the door, and the bell rang. Bahir's balding head popped up from behind the counter, and his crooked grin stretched across his wrinkled face. He peered at us with tired eyes as he shook his head.

"I'm sorry, we're actually closed for the evening. If you—"

"Dandelions are beautiful this time of year, don't you think?"

Bahir paled and tugged on the collar of his dark-red tunic. "Oh, umm, r-right this way."

We followed him through the array of flowers until we reached the back of the shop. Beyond that, I knew there would be a greenhouse, but we didn't go that way. Instead, Bahir opened a door and motioned for us to enter. I gave Marian one quick nod before stepping inside. Four walls surrounded us and nothing more. No doors or stairs or even a window. My heart thumped in my chest as panic settled in. Was this some sort of trap? Had Marian lured me in here to finally end me?

Before I could utter a word, the door slammed closed, and darkness encompassed us. A second later three lanterns flickered to life that hadn't been there a moment ago. The wall across from the door shimmered into nothing, revealing a staircase.

Magic, and good magic at that.

"Are you just going to stare at them or are you going to go down?" Marian said impatiently.

I made my way down the staircase, winding around and around, until the air grew thin, and the lantern-covered walls turned from red brick to cold dirt. The final step pooled out into another small broom closet. Shelves sat on either side filled with rags, buckets, and other odds and ends. Marian scooted around me and rapped her hand three times on a door along the back wall.

A large man opened it. He wore a thick gray tunic with the sleeves cut off and a pair of pants that were far too tight for his thighs. His balding head shone against the lantern's light as he narrowed his eyes on us.

"The day's flower?" he asked.

Without skipping a beat, Marian replied, "Dandelions."

The man stepped back, but what caught my eye behind him nearly had me stopping in my tracks.

Hundreds of men and women gathered in what appeared to be some sort of arena. Some were in rags as they walked around serving food and drink to the patrons. Rows upon rows of seats sat around an iron cage that reached the ceiling and took up the rest of the arena. Inside, what had everyone cheering and chanting, were some of the largest beasts I'd ever laid eyes on.

"What the hell are those things?"

"The queen's beasts." Marian said in a ravenous tone. Her fists clenched and her body stiffened as her eyes never wavered from the gruesome sight.

Black as night, the beasts ripped one another apart. A swipe of a paw had one beast crashing into the iron bars. It let out a yelp that sent the crowd cheering. I tugged Marian along as we made our way through the crowd. I needed to get a closer look. We found empty seats closer to the cage and sat down.

"Care for a beverage?" A woman in dark-blue rags lowered a platter of mugs. A small smile appeared on her face, one that felt far too forced. Bags under her eyes and sunken cheeks told me she wasn't being cared for. I balled my hands into fists.

"Yes, thank you," Marian said before taking a drink from the platter. She turned to me and whispered in my ear. "Remember why we're here, you have to blend in."

Right. Blend in.

I returned my gaze to the fight in front of me. Bright red eyes pierced through me as one of the beasts opened its giant maw and snapped at the other. They wrestled like two predators fighting for territory, ripping and tearing at each other. Blood coated the dirt beneath them, but neither of them quit.

My chest tightened and my stomach grew queasy. An assassin, born and bred to kill criminals who broke the queen's law, and yet I grew squeamish at the sight of two animals fighting for their lives. How could this be happening? Did the queen really know about this? Did she condone it? The woman who I'd pledged my eternal life to, who I'd killed for since I turned thirteen?

The crowd grew louder as they taunted the beasts. I panned around the room, taking in the faces of those who lived in the higher districts. The men and women whose riches helped fortify Chione. I recognized so many. The blacksmiths, the tailors, and even some of the queen's guards.

"How is it that none of the Brotherhood knew about this?" I gritted my teeth.

"How do you know that they all don't? The queen has a way of making you see only what she wants you to."

"How long has this been going on?"

Marian shrugged. "Months after the king's demise, I suppose."

So that meant she'd been doing this for *years*. This underground arena had been here for years, and I'd no idea. After the king's passing, Queen Gemma went into a deep depression and tended to disappear at night. A ruse so she could build all this. But why?

"These beasts, tell me about them."

Marian stiffened. "What do you want to know?"

"Everything. What are they, where did they come from, are they controlled by someone? I need to know what I'm up against here."

"Well, to answer your first question: they're villagers from the forest."

"I'm sorry, I don't think I heard you clearly over the chaos around us. Did you say these beasts are *people*?"

She nodded. "They're taken from their homes and brought here.

The queen figures it's better to take from villages outside the city where they're less inclined to retaliate. No one cares if someone goes missing from a poor village in the middle of nowhere."

For years I'd been complacent to a crime worse than anything I'd seen above ground. I wanted to scream, to unsheathe my hidden daggers and give justice to all those who thought of this as entertainment.

I tore my gaze from the destruction of the cage and went back to my search. Did the queen frequent this place? Hells, what would I do if she did? Killing my queen would be treasonous. Yet, I needed to figure out how to put an end to this.

"But then how—"

"She curses them. I don't know if you realize this since you seem to be pretty blind to her royal pain in the ass, but she's a witch."

I nearly let go of her arm.

"A witch?"

She nodded again.

"The queen of the fucking Enchanted Realm is a witch?"

"Keep it down," she hissed. "We don't need to draw attention to ourselves, remember?"

I rolled my eyes. "You think these people give a damn? They're too caught up in the show. All right, so she steals them and then curses them, but how does she keep them controlled?"

"It has something to do with the curse. Not only does she change them, but she binds them to her. Kind of like your fae bargains. Once the curse is in place, they're forced to obey her. I don't know how exactly, but when one of them is killed, or somehow the bond breaks, she knows."

To be bound to the queen until death. My heart hammered in my chest, my stomach turning. I'd recited the same vow when joining the Brotherhood. Bound to a life of servitude. Of course, we weren't cursed or physically bound. I could come and go as I pleased and had no ties to the queen other than my loyalty, but this … this was dishonorable.

"How does she keep them in line when she's not here, then?"

Marian's grip on my arm tightened. "She has the ability to give powers to whomever she deems necessary. The one who organizes this mess can only control them at night, otherwise they're locked away in cages."

"And how do you know so much about this?"

Marian slowly turned toward me, her eyes searching my face, and I found myself lost in the warmth of them. I shouldn't be here with her. I needed to bring her to the queen for the crimes she'd committed, and yet the desperation in her eyes stopped me. She needed my help. Not to be rescued or saved, just helped. Someone to understand the atrocities going on here. To believe her.

"Because I—"

A loud bell rang, pulling our attention back to the cage. One of the beasts lay motionless in the dirt. Blood pooled around a gaping wound in its side as the other paced back and forth alongside its body. Its sharp teeth were barred and covered in crimson.

A man walked into the cage, his arms raised as he made his way around the arena, and the cheers from the crowd died down.

"Ladies and gentlemen, we hope you're enjoying the show. Give a round of applause to Viper on yet another vicious victory."

The crowd exploded with applause. It made me sick.

"We have one last show for you before we bring this evening to an end."

I tuned the man out, unable to listen as he announced the next opponent. I'd come here to find out what the queen hid beneath the city, and we'd accomplished that. We needed leave, to regroup and figure out what to do next.

I stood to leave when my eyes caught a familiar face. A face that I'd seen every day. A face that shouldn't have been here.

An Elder.

"Rumplestiltskin?"

"What?" Marian followed my gaze.

"The man at the top of the stands. The one in gold robes."

He sat next to two women I'd seen around the castle. I squinted, and even from this distance I'd know those golden robes anywhere.

This man had dedicated his life to sitting on the council of Chione. To bring justice to the wrongdoings and to distribute the wealth around the city.

My feet moved before I could stop them. I weaved through the crowd. Blood pounded in my ears and my nostrils flared. Behind me Marian's voice snapped incoherent words, but I didn't care.

All I saw was red.

Until the crowd around me gasped. The noise stilling to nothing as the announcer said Marian's name.

"The Lioness has returned."

The Lioness?

I whirled around only to realize she stood feet from me, her arm no longer linked to mine. The illusion gone as Marian stood a few feet from me, a murderous glare on her face.

Shit.

I swore she'd be safe. Swore no one would recognize her so long as she kept her arm on my own. But in my anger, in my need to confront Rumple, I'd abandoned her.

Men dressed in armor swarmed her.

"Bring her forward, boys."

I took a step forward, but she shot me a look clearly telling me to stay put.

"Well, ladies and gentlemen, we have a treat for you today. The Viper will have new blood to spill. Place your bets now."

They carried her into the cage as the other beast barred their teeth and paced along the other side. Marian didn't kick, or buck, or put up any fight whatsoever. What's gotten into her? When I captured her, she fought my hold, she'd taken out dozens of people and nearly gutted a kingsman. I waited for her to do something—anything, but she didn't.

All around me, the crowd's voices grew into a crescendo of cheering I somehow managed to block out. My ears buzzed and chest tightened as I thought about what I could do to put a stop to this.

Marian found me one last time—a small smirk rose on her lips, and she gave one quick nod. She was a survivor, a warrior. She'd spent weeks out on the streets of Chione taking down ruthless men. From what I knew about her, she could handle her own. I just had to trust that she'd make it out of this. There were too many people, too many that may recognize me if I tried anything stupid. As much as it pained me to do so, I had to leave Marian's fate in her own hands.

The men released Marian and from one breath to the next, she shifted.

IV. THE LIONESS

MARIAN'S BEAST FORM WAS MAGNIFICENT.

Her bright red eyes surveyed their opponent. Marian—the Lioness—let out a high-pitched wailing cry that broke through the chants of the crowd. It sent unexpected shivers down my back and fear through my bones. My entire body froze where I stood, unable to comprehend the beauty and the beast in front of me. Huge—grizzly bear huge—she stalked around the cage, her massive paws stepping with methodical precision.

She's one of them. A human cursed by the queen for people's entertainment.

Shadow, much like my own, encased Marian in its grasp, fusing with long black fur that moved in breezeless air. Her gaping maw displayed razor sharp teeth, and her large pointed ears twitched with each move her opponent made.

A bell sounded, and the Viper leaped forward, but Marian dodged the attack with an elegance of a genuine assassin. Her paw smacked the other beast's side causing it to yelp. As long as Marian kept that speed up, she'd be all right. They danced back and forth, and as one lunged, the other dodged. So fast it seemed time had been sped up to make the fight move in a blur.

The Viper's paw struck Marian's jaw, and I winced. Marian shook herself, as if the hit hadn't phased her. The Viper may have been strong, but there was no question which beast was the nastier opponent. The Viper bled from a dozen small wounds and slowed down from fatigue I guessed had more to do with its last fight. Marian struck again, and a shallow cut stretched on the Viper's shoulder to its hip.

It yelped in pain, but Marian never let her eyes wander. The Viper had gotten a few good hits in too, one that bled from Marian's side—her coat thick with crimson—but neither of them let up.

Every part of me wanted to jump into that ring and put a stop to it, but my muscles would just not move. I sat there frozen as the two animals tore each other apart.

The Viper lunged forward, and Marian barely got out of the way. A tongue lopped out the side of her mouth as she panted. Before she could counterattack, the Viper's teeth snatched Marian's leg. She whimpered, thrashing, and bucking in an attempt to get the beast to let go.

Come on, Marian, you can do this.

Just as those words left my mind, the Viper's grip loosened and

Marian kicked, sending its body flying into the cage. A loud crack rippled through the arena. The limp body refused to move, save for the faint rise and fall of its chest. Marian teetered to one side but managed to kept herself upright. Once again, the crowd burst into cheers while I did my best to hold down my stomach.

How could so many people find this enjoyable? Fighting had always been meant for war, not for enjoyment. People cheered over Marian's badly wounded form and the Viper's near unconscious state. I wanted to jump from my seat and condone their behavior.

"End him," the announcer bellowed. *Or we will end you both.* I knew it to be true, those words. Why let a weak opponent live when the queen could just find more. Dozens of small villages stood throughout the forest, and with it dozens of potential victims.

My eyes widened as they returned to Marian. She didn't want to do this. I could see it in the flare of her red eyes, the way her ears pulled back and her tail curled between her hind legs. My heart ached for her, and yet she limped over to the Viper and placed her maw around the beast's throat. I kept my eyes forward, refusing to look away as bones crunched beneath Marian's grip. Again, the crowd cheered.

Barbarians.

"Take her to the back and clean her up boys, the Barron requests to see our little Lioness," the announcer said. "Now on to our main event."

I let his words fall to the side as I watched the cage open, and four men picked Marian up and carried her through the crowd and down a hallway. I couldn't let her out of my sight.

Weaving through the crowd, I chased after them. When I got to the entrance, I let smoke and shadow encompass me.

Dozens of tunnels connected in every direction. I followed the voices, but they grew more faint by the second. I tried to remember which direction they took as I turned down another tunnel, but it grew harder with each turn. I'd never been under the city before and finding my way through proved to be more difficult than I'd hoped. Every tunnel led to doors that led to empty rooms or more tunnels.

I was losing her.

I couldn't let that happen. Marian needed help and who knows what kind of physician they had down here. If they'd even take her to one. Maybe they had intended for the Viper to do the job for them? I pushed those thoughts to the side. Right now, I needed to find her and bring her back to Gretel—she'd be able to fix Marian up—and then after that we'd figure out a way to stop all of this. The queen would answer for these crimes against Chione, against the people of the villages she took her victims from. For Marian.

A large door engraved with symbols I didn't recognize stopped me in my tracks. I should have kept searching, but something in the back of my mind told me to go through. I shifted back to my human self and pushed open the door.

"What the hell?"

A hallway stretched for dozens of feet where cages sat on either side. Cages containing the same beasts from the arena. They all peered up at me, but none of them moved, none of them showed any sign of aggression. There were so many of them. People with lives and families who were probably worried about them. My teeth clenched nearly as hard as the hands at my side. I wanted to tear this place apart, burn it to the ground.

Now I understood why Marian had been hesitant to come back, why she spent her time hunting down the ones responsible. This had to be why the queen sent me on this mission to begin with. To capture the one who got away, to bring her back here, and I'd done it. I'd succeeded at returning her without even realizing.

I'm a fool. And now Marian would pay the ultimate price.

"Hey there, can any of you understand me?"

Marian said they were human once, cursed by the queen. Were they just the beast? Or had some parts of their human half remained? If I got one of them to speak to me, to tell me where Marian would have been taken, I could get to her before they did anything.

The beast closest to me turned and rested its head against its feet as it curled itself into a ball in the corner.

Maybe they couldn't speak in this form.

"Please, I need your help. They have my friend, and I need to make sure she's okay. Her name is Marian."

"You know Marian?"

I jumped and whirled around to the cage behind me. A naked woman stood behind the bars. Her pale skin dripped with sweat, and her red matted hair covered most of her face.

"Yes, she brought me here and we got separated after they spotted her. Do you know where they'd take her?"

"To the Barron."

"Yes, but where is that?"

"If you get me out of here, I can show you."

I shook my head. "That's too risky. I will release and save all of you, but right now Marian is in danger, and I can't afford to wait. I promise you I will get you out of here, but right now I need your help."

The woman considered me for a few seconds, her eyes trailing my length before she crossed her arms over her chest. "You're fae."

"Excuse me?"

"Give me your word, the word of the fae, that you will rescue us, and then I will tell you where the Barron is."

She hurried over and wrapped one of her hands around the bars while sticking the other out between them.

She wanted my word, a deal just as I'd given Marian. I'd promised her nothing would happen to her, that we'd just come and scope out the place, and instead I'd nearly cost Marian her life. I'd do anything to make that right.

"Fine. I promise to come back and rescue you so long as you tell me exactly where Marian is." My hand wrapped around her arm, and the magic did the rest. Once it finished, I took a step back to find that the rest of the beasts had moved to the bars of the cage, all eyeing me in a way that sent chills down my back.

"The Barron's quarters are a few corridors down from here. You'll want to take two lefts, a right, and then another left. You can't miss his door."

"How do you know all of this? Have you been here long?"

The woman nodded. "I arrived a week after the last full moon. The curse doesn't become permanent until the night of a full moon."

I nodded, still unsure how all of this worked, but I could ask Marian later. "Thank you. What's your name?"

"Aurora."

"Thank you, Aurora. I'll be back as soon as I can."

"You better," she said, peering down at her arm. "We're counting on you."

"Oh, one more thing: is there another exit? One that we can all escape from without going through the arena?"

"You come back for us, and I'll show you that too."

I gave a quick nod and hurried out of the room of cages and shifted back to the smoke before taking off down the corridors. I'd only been in the room for a moment, but who knows what could have been done to Marian in that time. As an assassin, we were taught different tactics when it came to torture. Getting information took time, and one could do a lot of damage. While I hadn't been one of the assassins who did the torturing, I'd been trained on how to do it. They'd punish her for escaping, for taking revenge on their people.

Two lefts, a right, and another left later, I stood before another grand golden door. This one had the same etching as the last, only it had two doors instead of one. At the center, engraved in the gold, sat a large snake coiled into a perfect circle around the door handles.

Muffled voices sounded from behind it. I shimmied my way down to the bottom of the door and squeezed myself through just enough so that my smoke wouldn't be noticed.

There were dozens of men in this room. All of them wore the same hoods as the assassins, as my brothers. A sick feeling swam in my stomach, and I fought the urge to shift and take down as many as I could. If these were from the Brotherhood, this entire operation ran deeper than I thought.

How had I been so blind to all of this?

Marian knelt in her human form in the corner of the room. Her clothes hunt from her body in shreds, and one of the guards held her matted hair in his fist. Blood dripped down her side from the earlier wound and her pale skin held traces of bruises. A gash on her lip and above her eye weren't any better. Though those appeared to be fresh.

Another man stood directly in front of her, and his hands kneaded together as I caught a glimpse of his red knuckles. He wore a black shirt and pants and a plethora of jewelry along his fingers and neck.

This must be the Barron.

"It's good to see you, Marian, or should I say, the Masked Maiden?" The man bent down until his face was level with Marian's and lifted her chin. "You cost us a lot of men and a lot more money. If you weren't so valuable to the queen, I'd kill you right here and now."

"Only a coward beats and murders women," Marian hissed.

The Barron struck.

Marian's head whipped to the side. I caught a glimpse of her as she bit her lip. Tears welled in her eyes as she fought from crying out. Anger nearly as potent as my smoke billowed through me. I wanted to rip him limb from limb. To tie him up and give him a taste of the pain he inflicted on these innocent souls.

The hold on my magic weakened. It wanted me to let go, to kill every single one of these men for sitting by and doing nothing. Right now, the best thing to do would be to get Marian out of here before any more harm could be done. But how? There were far too many guards in here to take all at once. Who knew if any of them had magical powers or were some sort of beast themself, especially if some of these men were from the Brotherhood.

I needed a distraction and fast.

Hang in there, Marian, I'll get you out of here.

Racing back toward the arena, I recalled every turn I'd taken to get to the Barron's room. Each tunnel I turned down fueled the fire burning inside me. The need to let it out, to bring down this entire place. A few minutes later, the chants grew louder, and finally the arena appeared. I shifted back before anyone noticed and ran back up the stairs and out of the flower shop. Sherwood greeted me with a snort.

"Sorry, boy, I'll be back for you soon."

I unhooked my bow and quiver from his saddle and threw the quiver over my shoulder. With one long inhale, I tossed my hood over my head and took off back inside. I ignored Bahir's shouts as I raced down the winding staircase. He'd learn soon enough what was about to be done.

The guard at the door shouted and cheered, far too distracted by the main event to notice me slip through. I kept to the far side of the arena. None of the patrons bothered to look in my direction—too busy consumed by the bloodshed of the cage—and I darted behind a pillar. Two beasts going at it like rabid dogs. I'd never understand why people found this enjoyable. Bile rose in my throat, and I fought to keep myself focused.

Nocking an arrow, I called on my gift, the fae magic linked to both fire and smoke, and watched as the tip of the arrow burst into flames. Taking a deep and controlled breath, I let go. The arrow soared through the air and stuck to the wall along the other side of the arena. One after another, in rapid succession, arrows flew from my bow. The entire place glistened with flames as panic set in the crowd.

"Fire!" they screamed.

Smoke engulfed the arena. Hundreds of people trampled over one another to get up the stairs. Their screams and cries carried over the room. I caught a glimpse of Rumple in the masses and grinned. While he probably would get out before the flames reached him, it still enjoyed watching the panic rise in his face.

Moments later, a dozen or so guards appeared through the tunnel. They undid their cloaks in what I knew would be a failed attempt to put out the fires. My magic wouldn't be so easily defeated.

Dropping my bow and quiver, I shifted and rose to blend in with the rising smoke. Left, then right, then left again, I made my way back through the tunnels. I'd tried my best to ensure I remembered how many lefts before a right, but I felt myself getting lost by the second. Panic rose in my chest and my throat tightened. How could I have been so stupid to think I'd be able to maneuver my way through here without getting lost again? Two lefts and then a right followed by two more lefts, or had it been a right first then a left?

After a few minutes of vigorous searching, I somehow managed to stumble upon the room of cages. Relief flooded through me as I recalled the mermaid's directions and found my way to the Barron's room. The doors were wide open.

"What the fuck did you do?" The Barron's voice thundered

through the tunnel.

"How could I possibly do anything when you have me tied up?"

"I will find out what you did, Marian, and once I do, the queen will be the least of your worries." The Barron turned toward his men. "Get out there and help them. If we must leave, lock this one up with the rest of them and let them burn. I don't give a damn what the queen says."

The last remaining guards shuffled out of the room and down the tunnel behind me. I focused my attention on the Barron. No protection? No leaving behind guards to cover him in case of an attack?

"Not really smart of you to send all your minions away when your precious arena is burning to the ground," Marian smirked.

"Not smart of you to start the fire and think you could actually get away with it."

Marian shrugged. "I'd love to take credit for this, but I'm pretty sure I'm the least of your worries right now."

"Is that so?"

I shifted once more, my magic and muscles tiring as I did. Shifting from human to smoke so many times in a row took a lot of energy, and I'd already used a lot of it disguising Marian and myself. As I emerged from my other self, the Barron jumped, his eyes wide as he realized who stood in his doorway. I'd never met this man before, never seen him on the streets or anywhere in the castle. He was shorter than me with unkempt golden hair and bright-blue eyes. His ears came to a point and his nose curled ever so slightly at the end.

"What are you doing here, Hood?" The Barron's voice deepened as he moved to stand between me and Marian.

"It appears you've broken many laws here, Barron. I'm going to have to take you in."

The Barron threw his head back and laughed. His whole body shook as he wiped a tear from his eye. "Oh, Hood, you have a lot of balls coming in here and spouting things about broken laws considering what you just did. Assuming the fire and smoke is your doing, of course."

"You have men and women locked up and caged, cursing them for entertainment, and you want to talk to me about what I did? I did this city a favor. Back away from Marian, and I'll consider killing you swiftly."

In reality, I wanted to tie him to one of the various chairs in the room, and cut into him inch by inch until nothing but blood coated his pale skin. While I wasn't one of the various assassins who tortured people, that didn't mean I couldn't do it. Although I preferred to leave that kind of stuff to those with darker souls, I wouldn't hesitate when it came to innocent lives. My fists clenched at my side, and I gritted my teeth.

Behind him, Marian worked to get herself free. She shot me a look, one with explicit instructions to keep her captor talking.

"You do know what I'm capable of, don't you?" I grinned. "What the Brotherhood has taught me? Considering you have a few assassins in your employment, I'd assume you do. If you've heard of me, you also know about my gift. Before long, the fire that's inside the arena will reach the tunnels. Have you ever experienced magical fire, Barron? Did you know it's unfazed by normal water? Only I, or a water fae, can put it out. Maybe" —I took a step closer— "if you let us go, I'll save you the trouble of calling a water fae and extinguish it myself."

With each step forward I made, the Barron took one back. Marian nodded once, freeing herself from the rope at last. I just needed to direct him back far enough, and she'd be able to knock him out.

"Y-you can't d-do anything to me, Hood. If the q-queen finds out, sh-she'll kill you."

"At least I'll die knowing I put a stop to this." I spread my hands out just as Marian leapt.

I'd expected her to knock him down with a chair or jump on him and hold him back. I should have known better. I should have known that the Masked Maiden wouldn't let this man go free.

The change from human to beast happened quickly. Her clothes shredded even more than they already were. Dark, crimson-soaked fur sprouted from her skin. Nails lengthened to claws and teeth elongated to a sharp point. The Barron didn't even have a chance to scream.

Marian's teeth sank into his neck, and he sputtered and gasped as his hands wrapped around Marian's maw. She gave one quick tug, snapped his neck, and then dropped his limp form on the hard floor.

Fury flickered through her bright red eyes as they left the Barron and turned toward me. Her body shuddered before sinking to the ground as the last of her energy faded. Seconds turned into minutes as she fought to shift back. Sweat covered her naked body as the change left her gasping for air. I unclasped my cloak and wrapped it around her before scooping her up into my arms. I turned toward the door, ignoring the motionless body of the Barron.

Smoke started to fill the halls as we exited. Marian coughed and placed part of the cloak over her mouth.

"We have one stop to make before getting out of here, okay? Just hang on."

Marian shifted in my arms until her face buried itself in my chest. Every part of her shook against me.

The door to the caged room remained shut, and it took every ounce of my remaining energy to not find and kill every last one of the guards.

Cowards were probably already gone.

How could they just leave all these poor souls to die? I turned and pushed the door open with a kick.

"You came back," Aurora's voice quivered.

"I do my best to keep my promises," I said as I put Marian down. Guilt rose in my chest as I took in her weakened frame. I'd promised to keep her safe, the bargain had been clear that no harm would come to her, and yet she sat there bloody, bruised, and nearly unconscious. I'd failed her. I'd never broken a bargain before, never went against my own word. What would the consequences of such actions be? I'd find out soon enough.

"Any idea on where they keep the key?"

"H-here." Behind me, Marian held up a single skeleton key. Her shaking hand barely kept it up as I rushed over to take it from her. "Don't ask, just free them."

And so I did. With each cage I opened, the beasts inside burrowed out of their hole. All of them giving me a nod or brushing against my leg in what I figured was thanks.

"Now," I said looking at Aurora as I gathered Marian back in my arms, "how do we get out of here?"

"Follow me."

V. CURSED SOULS

"YOU DID *WHAT?*" GRETEL SCREECHED. Her face darkened to a deep red as she fummed. "What in hells were you thinking?"

I wasn't, but she didn't need to know that.

A few hours had passed since we'd arrived just before sunrise with two dozen people stuck in their beast form. I still had no idea how Marian had been able to shift at will when these poor folks couldn't. Yet another question I'd ask her once she awoke. I'd only gathered a small amount of information from her in regards to the beasts, but with everything going on, I needed to know more. In order to help these people, to smuggle them out of a city brimming with assassins and guards, I needed to know what other possible threats awaited us.

"You and I both know these people needed help, and the only person I knew who'd keep their mouth shut would be you, Gret. We can't move them during the day—too many eyes—and I don't think any of them can shift on their own. I have to wait for Marian to wake up. Until then, they have to stay here. Please?"

Gretel's brows knitted together for a moment before she threw her hands up. "How can I say no to that? They can stay for the day, but, Hood, if someone comes asking questions—"

"I'll handle them."

"So, she really had these people fighting to the death?" Hansel chimed in. He took a bite of an apple, the crunch making my stomach knot. I nearly snatched the thing out of his hand before he threw one my way.

"Thanks, and yeah, I don't know much. She kidnapped people from villages on the outskirts of Chione. She curses them, which forces them to turn into some sort of beast, and then they're compelled to obey. Pitted against one another to fight for their life."

Those villages were filled with people who could barely afford to eat, and she stole them from their homes. Who knows how many children were left without parents, or spouses left to mourn their lover with no idea of what happened to them.

"And here I thought she was some sort of saint," Hansel said.

"You can't be serious?" Gretel scoffed. "Are you really that stupid, Hansel? Everything she does is fake. I know you work for her, Robin, but she's an evil son-of-a-bitch. Now that I know what she's been doing, I want to rip her cold, black heart out."

"Oh, I like her."

I jumped and nearly fell out of my chair as Aurora appeared. She'd since bathed and pulled her hair back into a bun leaving only a few strands against her face. She wore a plain white shirt and a pair of black pants that seemed far too large for her lanky limbs.

"Aurora, how are you?" I asked.

"Better, thanks to you."

"And everyone else?"

"I don't know. They won't be able to shift from their beast side until their bond to the queen is broken. So, it's hard to say."

"Breaking the bond. Would that also break their curse?"

Aurora shook her head. "Unfortunately, that part of the curse is permanent, but once they have the ability to shift back to human, they will be able to live a semi-normal life."

Gretel stepped in front of me, her gaze inspecting every inch of Aurora. "What are you?"

Aurora's lips curled into a tight grin. The two women stared each other down like feral cats, neither of them wanting to make the first move. Daggers, knives, and several blades covered Gretel from her boots to her hair; if she wanted to, she could drop Aurora in a second. I advanced forward, only for Gretel to stick her arm out to stop me.

"Hold on, Hood. I'm not going to harm her. I just want to know what she is."

Gretel's sense of smell had picked me out of a crowd before. Apparently all fae had an earthy smell with a hint of orange. She'd called me fae before we'd even introduced ourselves. But more than likely what Gretel smelled had more to do with the beast than anything else. Still, she could have been a bit nicer about it.

"And here I thought all the seekers were long since dead. Interesting to know my information is outdated," Aurora said. She placed a hand on her chest. "I'm a mermaid."

My body tensed as I staggered back, and I nearly bumped into Hansel, who'd somehow snuck up behind me. He wrapped an arm around my shoulder and took another bite of his apple.

A mermaid. I'd never seen one before. From the texts, mermaids had fins and gills and scales, not legs and feet to walk amongst the dry land. And what had she called Gretel? A seeker. What in hells was a seeker?

"How are you here if you're a mermaid?" Hansel asked.

"You mean because I'm walking on two feet? Mermaids are much more than humans give them credit for. But we all have our secrets, yes? Now, I can help you save these people, or we can stand here gaping at one another until we're all blue in the face."

I hadn't the faintest idea what sort of magic mermaids possessed. But, if we put all our combined efforts together, we'd get everyone to safety—that's what mattered.

"And how is a mermaid going to help us?" Gretel bit out.

Aurora peered around Gretel to look at me. "Did Marian not tell you how she managed to escape?"

We hadn't had much time to discuss much of anything. She'd come in and out of consciousness since leaving the arena. A wave of heat rose through me as dozens of questions rattled inside my mind. Marian's beast form flashed before my eyes. She was one of them, yet she'd been out of the arena for several weeks, and not once had there been a sighting of a beast. All her kills were done with a blade or by her hand. I hadn't even considered how she'd escaped until just now.

"We didn't have much time to discuss things with the place on fire," I said, shrugging Hansel's arm from my shoulders.

"Mermaids have unique gifts. You could equate it to the powers of a witch or a fae, but in reality, it's much more complex than that. Our magic comes from deep within the seven seas, given to us by a goddess. Because of this, we're able to counter many curses, heal many broken bones and wounds, and a few other tricks. Not all of us are the same, but every last one can break a bond given unwillingly."

Aurora had broken the bond between the queen and Marian. No wonder the queen ordered her capture. But it had nothing to do with the crimes she committed. Her pet beast escaped, and she had no way of controlling her or getting her back. Did Queen Gemma even know she had a mermaid in her cages? Or that a mermaid could break such bonds? I would never know, because after this I planned to leave Chione. I knew what that meant—I'd be breaking my own bond to my queen, to my brothers, and worst of all to the people—but I couldn't stay here. Not bringing Marian in would mean my own execution. If anyone in the arena noticed me, or caught a glimpse of me wandering the streets, the queen would find out. I'd have to leave with the rest of the beasts.

"Marian said that once the bond is broken, the queen will know. Will she be able to know where it happens? How are you going to break their bonds if the entire Brotherhood will be upon us within minutes?"

The Brotherhood's might shouldn't be taken lightly. I trained every day of every year with the Hoods. I knew their tactics, what they were capable of. Worry nipped at the back of my neck.

"Marian's right." Aurora picked at her cuticles." The queen will know, but it won't matter. She can't track the beasts; the bond doesn't work that way. She can detect when it's broken and maybe have a faint idea of where the broken bond took place, but that's it. And anyway, the Hoods and anyone else she sends won't be able to see us."

Gretel spun on her heels and faced me. Her face turned hotter than the sandy beaches of Chione. "You sure found a special one didn't you, Robin?"

"You are the Robin Hood who can shift his entire body into smoke, yes?" Aurora said, ignoring Gretel.

"Y-yes."

"Good, then we're all set. I suggest you get some sleep, Hood, you have a big job to do and will need your energy." Aurora gave a swift nod before strolling up the stairs and presumably to one of the empty rooms of the Inn.

"What in the hells was that about?" Gretel snapped.

"I wish I knew. Keep your eyes and ears open. I'm going to check on Marian and then take Aurora's advice. We'll move tonight when the city sleeps."

"Are you sure that's smart?" Hansel threw his apple core onto the desk before hopping over it. "Won't the guards and assassins still be wandering the streets?"

He had a point. The queen will want answers for what happened at the arena, but Aurora seemed not at all worried about them, and right now she was the only hope we had. Maybe speaking to Marian would shed some more light on the matter.

Marian looked much better than our last encounter; apparently the curse allowed for faster healing abilities. Most of the bruises were a light yellow and, save for the gash on her side, she appeared mostly healed. I'd found her in Gretel's spare room with a platter of meats and the tallest mug of ale Hansel owned. She shoved food in her mouth ravenously, something I'd see from a bear after hibernation than a human. I sat there patiently as she finished, not wanting to interrupt for fear of finding one of her blades at my throat. Though that wouldn't last long when my own stomach groaned in protest.

"Here," Marian said, shoving food in my direction. "There's plenty here for both of us."

I gave her a look that went unnoticed and plucked a piece of meat from her platter. A part of me melted the second the food touched my tongue. Juicy and savory and exactly what I needed. I must have made a noise because Marian laughed.

"And here I thought men only moaned like that in bed."

I coughed, nearly choking on the food. Catching my breath I said, "Well, I don't think I've tasted women as good as this."

She smirked. "Maybe you just haven't found the right one."

I froze, my throat tightened, and my stomach twirled—but not from hunger. Though, the hunger I felt now was much, much different. Marian's face flushed, and she quickly returned to her food.

Gods, this woman amazed me. A breath of fresh air that I didn't know I needed. She warmed something in me that not even Hansel and Gretel managed to do. Yet, a dark cloud still hovered around her, a telling sign that the darkness I'd felt earlier during our bargain had been something else entirely. The beast, the curse, it had all created this darkened aura around her. If I hadn't taken the chance to help her, I'd have never found out about the pits. I'd have never met this woman who was fiercer than most of the assassins I knew.

"I'm sorry," I said with a quiver in my voice.

"For what?"

"I promised you an apology. You were right about the arena, about the queen, about all of it. But most of all … I failed you. I promised that no harm would come to you, and I broke the bargain."

Marian shook her head. "You didn't break the bargain. The damage and harm done had nothing to do with you, Robin. You didn't force me to fight or take me from my home. So, don't think any of this is your fault, okay? It was only a matter of time before I had to enter that place again anyway. Plus, I'm pretty sure if we broke the bargain, you'd burst into flames or something."

She had a point, then again, I'd never broken one before, so I had no clue what to expect. Still, she'd practically begged me to allow her to stay behind, and I denied her that. I promised to keep her safe.

I opened my mouth to object, but she held up a hand. "Save it. I'm fine, and we're both alive. Now ask me the questions I'm sure you've been dying to ask."

A change of subject. Good.

"Why can't the queen track the beasts? You'd think a witch who can curse someone would want to know where their assets are at all times."

"Everything has limits, even magic. As I said before, the curse changes you from human to beast. It binds you to her so that you'll obey her every command. It doesn't allow her to track their every movement. It's why she kept us in cages so we couldn't escape. Why else do you think she had you hunting me for so long?"

I flinched and looked away, unable to meet her eyes. The queen had fooled me, made me believe the evil seeping in Chione belonged to Marian, a criminal who needed to be prosecuted at the highest level. If I'd have taken her to the queen, if I'd never allowed her the chance to show me the arena, I'd have brought a terrible fate upon her. I knew the queen and the punishments she'd inflicted. While rumors floated around that King Roland of Khan had a guillotine that his people feared, the queen had something much worse.

She had a brotherhood of assassins.

She had *me*.

An enforcer who'd gotten every criminal to confess their sins without a bat of an eye or a word of indignation. I'd allowed her to use me in her games. The Queen of the Enchanted Realm was the true evil soaking through the streets of Chione.

I cursed. How could I leave this city while she continued ruling it?

In that moment I knew, I knew I couldn't leave. These people needed someone who could save them. I'd have to disappear for a while of course, at least until the name Robin Hood had died on the tongues of the people.

"Are you okay?" Marian asked.

"My entire life has been a lie. Everything I've ever believed in, everything I've worked for, has been a tale told by a woman who gets off on pitting helpless people against one another for entertainment. So no … I'm far from okay. I don't even know who I am anymore." I rubbed my hands over my face, unable to bring myself to look at Marian just yet. What she must think of me, of the man who had willingly signed up to be a front for a terrible queen.

A pair of warm hands grabbed my wrists and lightly tugged them from my face. Marian knelt in front of me, and her eyes shimmered in the soft light illuminating the room. The warmth from her hands cascaded down my arms until every part of my soul beamed with that same shimmer. In that moment, with her hands around mine and our eyes locked, I felt like I could do anything, that I could *be* anything. My stomach fluttered in restless waves.

"I do. I've known you for a very short time, Robin, and in that short time, I've seen a man who gives a damn. A man who sacrificed everything to save someone he barely knew, to save an entire room of people he'd never met before. You could have left when I was taken, walked right out the door, and never looked back. But you didn't. And when you watched me kill the Barron, you scooped me up and carried me out of that place without a second thought. Most people would have run for the hills, but not you."

Tears welled in her eyes as she loosened her grip around my wrists. "What I see is someone with a heart and a soul—a good man. I always thought the people who belonged to the Brotherhood were vile, murderous, cold-hearted men. Yet here you sit, defeated and confessing your sins to me. I'm not one of the gods who demand you bear your truths to. I can see you're more than you let on, and I'm grateful you attacked me that day at the docks."

"You kicked me in the groin," I deadpanned.

Marian's laughter filled the room, full of warmth and a sweetness that sent shivers down my back. I'd never heard something so beautiful before, and I never wanted it to stop.

Through gasps of breath, she said. "I-I'm … s-sorry."

"Don't worry, I'm sure everything still works."

Marian wiped the tears from her eyes and rubbed her cheeks. "Good, we wouldn't want those terrible tasting women to miss out."

The banter continued a while after. The two of us laughed until our stomachs ached. I'd never felt so comfortable in someone's presence before, yet Marian managed to make me forget about everything going on outside of the room.

"What are you going to do when you leave?" I asked.

"Oh, I'm not leaving," Marian said sharply. "There's a lot more to be done. Do you really think she won't start up again? That just because we took down her operation she won't try to rebuild? There are people out there in danger, and I can't sit by and let her hurt more innocent victims. I will continue to do everything in my power to put an end to her rule. I won't stop until one of us is killed."

Marian rose from the floor and strolled over to the window. She lifted the curtain slightly and shook her head. "I understand if you want to get out of this place, but I can't."

"You can't do this all by yourself, Marian. The Brotherhood will find you and take you down. The chances that you'll find another willing assassin are slim to none. Those men are ruthless, and they don't care. Some might, I know of a few with a softer heart, but they'll be much harder to sway."

"I don't give a damn. I refuse to stop. My mission is clear: I'll save as many lives as I can in exchange for my own. My soul is already tainted and full of hate and despair. There's nothing left for me in this world besides putting a stop to the queen."

The sadness in her tone, the slumping of her shoulders. Defeat. She really thought she'd have to do this alone.

"You said that I'm a good man, a man with a good heart and a soul. But you have a good heart and soul too. You sacrificed so much to help the beasts sleeping in the rooms of this Inn. You did everything in your power to give them their lives back. But you can't do this alone, and you won't."

Marian shot me a look. "What are you saying?"

"I'm saying that I'm staying with you. I know Chione, I know the Brotherhood, and the queen. We can do this together. We can stop her together."

Marian gaped at me, her jaw slack and her eyes wide in disbelief. "Y-you really mean that? You'd do that?"

My heart raced as I moved to the window. I shoved my hands into the pocket of my pants, hoping she wouldn't notice how badly I wanted to touch her. To wrap my arms around her and feel her against me. The moment we locked eyes for the first time something sparked within me; seeing her here, fighting for what she believed in was courageous and inspiring and I had no idea how to feel about any of it.

"If you want to stay and fight and end this, then I'm not going anywhere. I'll stand with you, Marian. After all, I have no one else either. No one to care for and no one to care for me. All I've ever known is how to be an assassin, so why not put that to good use?"

Marian remained frozen where she stood. Her lips trembled and a hand rubbed the back of her neck. I wished then that my fae magic had granted me the gift of telepathy. Did she want me to step closer? Did she want me to leave? Her face gave away nothing but shock and perhaps unease. I couldn't be certain.

"You're wrong," she finally said.

"About what?"

Marian closed the short distance between us. She smelled of freshly picked flowers and something fruity. The scent wrapped around me, grabbing me in its hold as she brought a shaky hand to my cheek. Once again, her touch sent a warmth through me, a spark of energy that told me I could take on the world with her by my side.

"You have one person who cares about you now."

She lifted to her toes and brushed her lips against mine. Her warmth, mixed with the scent of fruit, had me shuddering against her. The feather-light kiss came and went, and I was left … stunned.

She kissed me.

She *cared* about me. *Me.*

I cleared my throat. "Marian, I—"

She stepped back, wide eyed and face reddening as she shook her head. "Sorry, I shouldn't have … I didn't mean …"

I raised a brow. Was she shaking?

"Marian." I stepped closer, but she shook her head again.

"Let's just get this over with, and then we can talk, okay? Get some sleep, and I'll wake you when it's time." Marian hurried out of the room. She closed the door, leaving me alone to my racing thoughts and beating heart.

VI. A QUEEN'S ASSASSIN

THE TOUCH OF MARIAN'S SOFT LIPS ON MINE LINGERED as we parted ways. I hated the idea of us all breaking off into individual groups, but Gretel and Marian agreed it was smarter just in case any of them were caught; at the very least those who weren't would be able to reach the forest without problems.

It still didn't mean I had to like it.

Hansel and Gretel took the smallest group through the Market district. While traveling that way posed a risk, the two of them were well known and loved throughout that part of Chione. No one would question the twins. Not when they kept most of those businesses afloat. Marian and Aurora took their larger group along the shores as soon as night fell, while my group had to travel through the heart of Chione—the VonWhite district. The VonWhite was the royal family name. A name honored with statues and tributes and the occasional celebrations.

My group moved as one; smoke weaved and curled its way between bodies as we headed toward the city's center. The smoke would keep us all hidden, and with the intense cloud cover and fog already rolling off the shores, we'd be impossible to spot. As long as everyone remained linked, we'd get through the district and to the forest before anything happened.

I tried to shove away the impending doom that wrestled in my chest. That evil pit in my stomach that told me everything was going to go wrong. By now, Hansel and Gretel would be returning to the Inn, and Aurora and Marian would be reaching the shore. Everything would be fine, yet something still felt so terribly wrong.

Then again, the feeling had started after watching the mermaid break the bond from each beast. The screams and cries and pleads for death were unbearable. Though the second the bond broke, Aurora had been flooded with thanks, hugs, and even kisses.

Once the beasts were relatively free, that's when things got real. My mind opened back up to that final conversation:

"From the second the bond is broken, she'll know. She'll send every guard and assassin to find us. We'll have to move fast." Marian grabbed my hand. "You know if she finds out what you're doing, about what you did, she'll hang you too. You may be her assassin, but she won't stand for disobedience."

The thought of her punishment crossed my mind a time or two. I didn't care. If she killed me, no one else would care either. Maybe Hansel and Gretel, and I suppose Marian too, but I'd gladly sacrifice myself in their name. I'd take their involvement with me to the afterlife. So long as everyone was safe, I would die with honor and possibly a shred of happiness.

I ran a finger over Marian's knuckles and smiled. "I'm more concerned about what she will do to you when she finds you. Be safe."

"You too. After all, we have a lot to talk about when this is all over." Marian winked before setting off with her group.

The memory dissolved in my mind as we entered the VonWhite district. The massive courtyard extended hundreds of feet in every direction. Stone statues sat in a circle in the middle, one for each god and goddess, the world's creators. At the center stood a much smaller statue, yet just as beautiful. Two young boys, their hands linked with one another as their foreheads pressed together. One, a bit taller with a crooked nose and a necklace around his neck, and the other no more than a few feet tall with curly hair and a smile on his face.

King John and Queen Sydney's children.

I knew the words at the foot of their statue. A story of a family whose fate ended in tragedy—one of pain and anguish and death.

Those poor boys.

A hand tightened around mine, pulling me from my thoughts. A squeeze that nearly cut off my circulation. I turned around to the woman beside me, her face white and full of panic.

"It's okay, we'll be out of the district before you know it," I said.

"I wouldn't be so certain." Her voice lowered to a whisper. "I can smell them."

While the bond to the queen had been broken, the curse would remain. Though, that part hadn't seemed to brother Marian as much.

She'd been able to smell breakfast from four rooms down and knew exactly what Gretel prepared. Blueberry muffins, orange juice, and fresh baked bread. If this woman could smell people approaching, it probably meant one thing.

The Brotherhood was near.

Thankfully the fog had picked up since our entry, but my smoke appeared a bit darker than normal fog. If any of them recognized it, if they came to inspect, I worried they'd see through it. Most of them knew about my gifts, but few of them ever saw it in action. Queen Gemma made sure of that.

One by one, assassins appeared along the rooftops. All of them hooded and their faces shrouded in darkness. Once more, the dark pit in my stomach ached and grew into a beating heart while blood pounded in my ears.

I had to keep these people safe.

I turned so everyone could see me and held a finger to my lips. None of us moved, none of us dared speak as we waited to see what the assassins would do.

"You see that, Carter?" a familiar voice sounded from above.

"Yeah, kind of looks darker, don't you think?"

Oh gods. I'd failed them.

The Brotherhood had spotted us, and at any second they'd attacked, jumping down from their perches and firing upon us.

"Maybe go down there and get a better look."

I sucked in a deep breath and shook my head at the people in my care.

"I'll handle this," I whispered.

Carter, a newer recruit, stood and made his way to the edge of the roof.

Boom.

Everyone jumped at once as the sound echoed through the sky. Moments later, hues of red and orange colored the otherwise darkened sky.

Boom.

Another one. What in hells was that?

"It's the docks!" an assassin yelled. "They're on fire."

"That must be them. Go, now!"

One by one, the assassins leapt, disappearing into the night. A weight lifted from my shoulders. Time to move.

Whoever aided in our escape needed a night's worth of free drinks. For now, I just needed to get these people out of Chione while we still had the chance.

"Eddard?" I asked and shoved a piece of bread into my mouth.

Hansel laughed. "Yep, apparently Gretel took it upon herself to get some help, just in case. According to Eddard, he just wanted to"— Hansel dropped into a mocking tone— "'blow shit up and not have to clean up the mess.'"

I shook my head and smiled. While that had been great and gave us the distraction we needed to get the hells out of Chione, we still hadn't heard anything from Aurora and Marian.

I rubbed my brow and tried to tell myself that Marian would make it back. I'd seen her fight, and Aurora had tricks up her sleeve that even I couldn't comprehend. They'd be fine. They *had* to be fine.

"Robin, you okay?" Gretel asked.

I nodded. "Just worried."

"About your cute little friend?" She raised her brow and smirked as she wiped an empty mug.

Rolling my eyes, I set my own mug down and popped another piece of bread into my mouth.

"Aurora said their journey would be much longer. It could be well into tomorrow before we see them. Just be patient and get yourself some rest. I'll come get you the moment they return."

How was I going to sleep knowing they were still out there? But if I planned to be any use when they returned, I needed to try. I'd done a lot the last few days with minimal rest. I'd just have to close my eyes for a bit and when I woke up, Marian would be back, and all would be well.

Giving a wave, I retreated to my room.

My head throbbed, and every muscle in my body protested each step. I'd made it to my room just in time to crash. Falling on the bed, I smothered my face into the pillow and hoped with everything I had that Marian and Aurora would be all right.

They had to be. They'd get the others far away from Chione and be back in no time. I had to believe that. And yet, an overwhelming sense of dread trickled through my senses, digging in the pit of my stomach like sewer rats. No matter how many times I forced myself to think happy thoughts, a darkness clouded over them.

My mind raced as I lifted my head from the pillow. The hair on the back of my neck stood on end, and gooseflesh rolled down my skin. Was this my subconscious telling me they didn't make it? That I'd been foolish to think they were all right? I sat up and cursed the darkness surrounding me.

Closing my eyes, I searched my gift in hopes it would tell me something more. Though my aching body and tired eyes made it near impossible to focus.

Come on, Robin.

My magic, the ancestral blood of the fae that swam through my veins was always so potent and raw. Now, something blocked it. A barrier that refused me access to what I wanted. I lowered myself back onto the pillow and let out a long, deep breath. How was I going to sleep when my own magic grew restless?

My grandmother, the woman who'd spent my entire life taking care of me, would have made me a cup of her famous lemon tea and sang to me until I finally drifted off. Here, in the quiet of the Inn, I had nothing but the breeze from the open window to keep me company. That and footsteps… several footsteps.

I grabbed for my dagger when the door to the room flung open, and I shot upright. The light from the hall filtered in, giving me a glimpse of my intruder. I blinked once, then twice, but nothing changed. Sharp dark eyes pierced through me. Wisps of gray threaded through locks of black hair that had been pulled up and away from their face. Deep red lips pulled into a tight smile giving away wrinkles along rosy cheeks and in the corners of eyes. The last person I wanted to see.

The queen.

She stood in the doorway, two guards at her back and a man in a hood. A hood I knew very well. My fists clenched around the linens of the bed, and my eyes widened while my chest tightened.

No.

This wasn't happening. I'd been careful, I made sure no one saw me enter the Inn. I'd double checked, went back the way we came and made sure we missed all the patrols. Or so I thought I had, yet her minions somehow found me. I'd been doing this a long time, keeping to the shadows, but perhaps a large number of random wolf-like dogs traipsing around the city drew more attention in the night than I would have thought. I'd used my magic, but obviously I'd missed something.

It didn't matter how she found me, what mattered now was finding out why. Had Hansel and Gretel heard the queen enter their Inn? Were they safe?

"Queen Gemma, wh-what a surprise. What are you doing here?"

I centered myself, doing my best to not anger the witch queen. I wondered … could my weakness, my block in magic, had it been her doing? I didn't know the extent of her power, and today surely wasn't the day to find out.

"Well, Robin, I could ask you the same thing. You haven't reported to your Elder in a few days. We were beginning to worry the Maiden got the best of you," she said as she shut the door behind her, leaving the others to stand guard.

"Apologies, My Queen. The Maiden has not been easy to find and even harder to capture. I can give him an update if you want to let

Elder Wulfe in."

I bit my tongue and prayed she didn't see through my lies. My mind reeled, dozens of questions as to how she found me, how she knew I'd be here.

"Oh, that won't be necessary."

I raised a brow. "Well, I'm sure—"

Queen Gemma lifted her hand to silence me. "I'm sure he will want to hear about everything you've done these last few days. But that's not what I'm here for."

Sweat gathered along my brow as my heart raced. Panic overwhelmed me, catching me in its hold as it pricked and tugged at my nerves. Something wasn't right. Did she know? Had she found out about what we'd done?

"Then why are you here, My Queen?"

"You'll be happy to know the Maiden has been apprehended."

Marian. She had Marian. My nails dug into my skin as red hot fire burned within me. How did this happen? How could I have let this happen? I shouldn't have left her. No matter what Aurora thought, I could have handled everyone in my smoke. We'd all have made it out and back again without a problem. The queen may have still found me, but at least Marian wouldn't have been caught. How did she even know where to find her? There's no way she knew of our plan. We'd been careful. Hadn't we?

"Her and a band of criminals made an attempt to flee the city."

Criminals.

Those innocent people she stole from their homes were criminals?

For years, I'd considered Queen Gemma to be one of the noblest to sit on a throne. She always seemed to care about her people in Chione. She'd worked tirelessly to give back to the poor. I'd witnessed her generosity with my own eyes. Passing out food to those who starved, giving coins to a little girl who just wanted a new doll. Had all of it been for show? A ruse to make people believe she actually gave a damn? The criminals she referred to flashed in my mind's eye. The same people who were forced to fight to the death, who were stolen from their families and cursed to live a double life. I wanted to scream, to bring Gemma out to the people and tell them what kind of person ruled their city. But they wouldn't believe me. No one would believe me. I was a fool to think anyone would believe the word of an assassin compared to that of a queen.

I'd failed, and this time I had no idea how to fix it.

"Well good; then I suppose my job here is done."

That's it, Robin, play stupid to the queen.

Internally my eyes were rolling to the back of my head. What a stupid thing to think.

"Come now, Robin, you can stop with the ruse. I know more than you think, but what I don't know, what I seem to not understand, is why you've betrayed your queen?"

"I have no idea what you're talk—"

"*Don't* play me for a fool, Hood. Tell me why you defied me. I want the truth."

She wanted to know the truth. I nearly laughed out loud. Did she think I was stupid? That she didn't know the vile things she did? She really expected me to let that slide, to sit back and let innocents be victimized by her. No. Not anymore. Not if I had anything to say about it.

"You're a witch. You cursed hundreds, possibly thousands of people for entertainment. You make them fight to the death. Anyone who condones murder is a coward."

Gemma shot forward. The air grew thick as she approached. "Did you just call me a coward? A boy who hid under the stairs of his home and watched his family be slaughtered?"

I stilled. My mother and father. My brother. She hadn't been there, hadn't seen their bodies bloodied and beaten to death. I know because it was only me for days upon days, hiding until people started to worry about us. I'd been starving and wishing death upon myself when our neighbor walked in. He'd been the only one who knew. Or so I thought.

"How did you know?"

The queen threw her head back and laughed, the eerie noise sending gooseflesh along my skin. "Still that naive little boy. I see everything. I *know* everything. I know you set fire to my establishment. You didn't kill Kline, that was the Maiden, but you did release my prisoners. I have eyes and ears everywhere. Just like I know this is the place where you lay your head when you're not at the castle."

My vision blurred. She knew it all. Had we been betrayed? Hansel and Gretel would never tell the queen anything. No matter how much she tortured them. I didn't want to believe it had been Marian. My lips tingled with the faint reminder of her kiss and the promise it left behind.

That only left Aurora. But she'd helped me get the prisoners out, she made sure …

Fuck.

She'd been with Marian. I hadn't questioned her when she said she'd take care of the Maiden. Still, it didn't seem right. Why would she help us, then? Why would she have helped Marian escape in the first place? None of this added up.

I had to be missing something.

"I see the wheels in your brain trying to figure out how I knew. And you'll continue to guess and still be wrong no matter how much you think about it. That little bit of information will be shared at the right moment. Anyway, you should waste your energy on something else. Or *someone* else."

I kept my feet planted and forced myself to stay rooted. I may have wanted to do things I promised myself I'd never do, especially to the queen, but I needed to know what she'd done with Marian. I had to fix this.

"What have you done with her? I swear if you've hurt her—"

"You've grown feelings toward this girl, haven't you?"

I furrowed my brows. There were no guards in here, no one to stop me if I were to grab my dagger and slit her throat. But for Marian's sake, I couldn't do that. I had to fight for her, and to find out where the queen took her.

First, I had to figure out how to get myself out of here.

"By that silence, I'll take that as a yes. Good, because that will make this next part really fun."

"Next part?" I asked.

"You see, I know you better than you think. I know how much

innocent lives matter to you, the little people. You care more about them than you ever did me. Which is why I know you'll behave. Which is why you'll want to listen to this next part very carefully if you want your Masked Maiden to live."

All my attention, every breath and heartbeat, latched on to her words.

"Your set of skills is very impressive. Irreplaceable, some might say. I'd have to agree, which is why I'm willing to give you one last chance."

A chance. In all my years of service to the queen, she'd never given anyone a second chance. My smoke, my gift, really must have been important to her. The queen didn't spare lives unless she had an ulterior motive, and willing to spare my life—Marian's life—after what we did, she must really be desperate.

I stilled. Was this all some trick? Had she planted this entire scheme to ensure my fealty? No. That didn't make sense. I was already loyal to her. I'd spent almost all my life believing in her.

"But let me make this very clear. You will never see your pretty little friend again. So long as you do as you're told, so long as you never take a step out of line again." Queen Gemma took a final step forward until we were inches apart. Earth mixed with something bitter filled the air between us and I nearly gagged. She'd always smelled of mint and berries, not *this*. This wasn't the same queen I'd always known. "She will live out the rest of her days. But the moment you try to cross me, the second you think you're going to try and betray me again, I will find out, and I will kill her, and everyone you've ever cared about, without hesitation."

Queen Gemma was willing to spare Marian. One of her prisoners and fighters, someone who escaped her cages just so I would stay obedient. So, I would continue to be used as a pawn in whatever game she played. I'd never seen that before, this vicious side of her, and every part of my soul wanted to end her here and now.

The queen was smart. She wouldn't say any of this unless she'd covered all her bases. She'd never tell me Marian's whereabouts, but I had connections and people who'd be able to find her. I'd play my part and be the good little assassin she wanted me to be, pretend to forget about Marian and do what needed to be done. But I wouldn't stop trying to find her. I'd find a way to take down the queen, to beat her at her own game. She was methodical and cunning. But I was an assassin, a killer, a *hunter*. Marian may have gotten me into this mess, but it was up to me to clean it up.

"All I have to do is follow your orders completely and Marian will be unharmed?"

A wicked grin pulled on the queen's lips. "*Marian*." She said her name with such surprise. Had she not known her real name? "And yes, that's it. Nothing more, nothing less."

"I want to know that she's alive first."

Queen Gemma walked over to a small oval mirror hanging on the wall and waved her hand over it.

A black ball of fur shimmered into view. Her ears perked up as she looked around—Marian in her beast form. When she didn't see anyone, she curled herself back into a ball.

Darkness surrounded her in waves, save for a sliver of moonlight through a barred window. I saw nothing else to help identify her location. Though, the moon told me wherever the queen placed her, it wasn't anywhere near the Enchanted Realm. How far away had the queen taken her? And how did she do it so fast?

Marian was alive. I didn't know for how long, and for all I knew, the queen could have her killed the second I agreed to her terms.

Unless …

Realization hit me. Did this mean… hells, was the queen about to ask me for a bargain? If she did, at least I knew Marian would be safe so long as I did what I needed to. It would make things much harder, but I'd figure it out.

"You want a bargain?"

Nodding, she held out her arm. My eyes trailed down to her open palm.

"To ensure we will both keep our word."

"One last thing I need to know. What did you do with the other *criminals*?"

"I thought Marian could use the company."

She had them locked away too?

"Pity we couldn't find them all. But no matter, there's plenty more where they came from."

Hells, Robin, how did you not realize the depths of this woman's darker side?

Not having a choice, I clasped my hand around her arms and let the smoke wrap itself around us.

The queen let go as soon as the smoke vanished.

"Good, now I have to see a certain Innkeeper about a guest she has. The kingsman and I have much to discuss. Do see to it that you return to the castle promptly." Turning on her heels, the queen strode to the door and opened it. Three guards and an Elder stood on the other side.

Wulf. He didn't even look my way as Queen Gemma took his arm and disappeared down the hall.

I let out a lengthy breath and hoped Hansel and Gretel wouldn't be punished for their help in this matter. They were good people, and if the queen were smart, she'd leave them mostly unharmed.

Defeated, I fell back on the bed. This was going to be a long, vigorous game of plucking the right pieces out of a puzzle. The better I played my part, the easier it would be to get what I wanted.

I rubbed my hands together, and a single tear fell down my cheek.

"I will find you, Marian. I won't stop until everyone responsible for your capture is taken down."

My magic wrapped itself around me, consuming me into a puff of smoke. It was time to get to work.

EPILOGUE

Marian

WAKE UP.

The voice in my head caused me to jolt upright. I cursed the damned gods at my throbbing head and aching limbs, then opened my eyes to complete darkness, not a stroke of light anywhere. Where was I?

Rolling to my knees, I pressed my hands against the cold hard floor. I hissed as something sharp dug into my skin—a rock? I wiped the hair away from my face, and took in a deep breath, but without being in my other form, I had no chance of deciphering any scent.

What happened? How did I get here?

My mind was an empty vessel of … nothing … no memory, no knowledge of what caused me to be here.

A cold breeze wrapped around me, and I shivered. A draft meant a door, or a window had to be nearby. Just as I tried to move, a door flew open, and I hissed as light flooded the room.

"Marian! Oh goody, you're awake," a small, high-pitched voice said.

I covered my eyes and tried to peer between my fingers to get a better look, but all I saw was a small frame to go with the small voice.

"I worried the blow to your head may have been a little too much. You'll start to feel better soon, though. Promise."

Hells, she sounded like a little girl.

"What happened? Where am I?" I said, my throat dry and voice groggy.

"Oh, you know, just your typical fun. Things burn to the ground, someone gets angry, the other person gets in big trouble, the mad one takes their revenge, and well, now you're here."

Shit.

It all came flooding back. The queen, being held against my will, escaping and getting my revenge. Robin. His tender care of me and the worry in his eyes when we were going our separate ways. The kindness in his eyes when he spoke to the rest of the beasts. A kindness I'd never known before, even before I'd been captured.

Everything had gone to plan, or so I thought it had.

"Marian, do you remember the conversation we had before I helped you escape the first time?" Aurora asked, the vision of our last conversation flooded my mind.

"You told me in order to save the others, I had to save myself first."

Aurora nodded. We'd been walking along the shores of Chione for an hour already, the others becoming increasingly impatient the longer we were out here. I'd reassured them several times that so long as they were in our care, we'd be fine. Aurora was an amazing mermaid with skills that trumped most fae. I didn't have any idea where she'd come from, but we were beyond glad to have her with us.

"I also gave you another reason. Do you remember?"

I nodded. A daughter who needed her, who would die if Aurora didn't get back to her."

Aurora peered over at me. "Well, I may have left out a few … details."

"What do you mean?"

Rustling in the trees pulled me from Aurora's smirk-filled lips. One by one gasps erupted around us as men of the Brotherhood appeared through the thick greenery, their swords pulled or bows aimed. My heart sank, and dread surrounded me in waves as the people around me stepped back. All of them turned their gazes on me. Surprise, shock, and betrayal littered their faces. They'd put their trust in me, their faith and lives, and now here we were. The assassin's boxed us in until we all stood back to back.

All except Aurora.

"Aurora, wh-what is this?"

Aurora raised her hand and snapped her fingers as a puff of smoke twirled around her and vanished just as fast. Behind the smoke stood someone else, someone other than the Aurora I knew.

White hair, pale skin, and a triumphant smile on her face, this woman was definitely not who I thought. She changed her appearance—a snap of her fingers and an entirely different person stood before me.

"The name's Ursa, my dear. The best sea witch in all the seven seas. Surely, you've heard of me?"

I had. Well, most of them were rumors really, but none of them were … none *of them were good.*

"Y-You're not a mermaid?"

Ursa laughed. "Not exactly, but I play the part well, don't I?"

If she wasn't a mermaid, how'd she break my link to the queen? How had she broken the link to several of the beasts?

"How is that possible?"

"A witch never reveals all of her secrets, but let's just say the magic of illusion is a tricky thing."

Illusion? My mind flashed back to a man with sandy blond hair, beautiful eyes, and a smile worth all the gold in Chione. Robin had masked my identity right before my eyes. So, Aurora—no, Ursa—had done the same?

"What do you want with me?"

"Nothing you can give, unfortunately." She unbuttoned her cloak, opening the sides to reveal another surprise, another twist to this awful fucking day.

"Your child is—"

"Not yet born. But once she is"—Ursa rubbed her belly—"she is going to be a power all on her own. A beautiful mermaid with the powers of a witch."

Another smirk pressed to Ursa's face as she continued to rub her belly. A daughter of both mermaid and witch. I'd never known many crossbreeds with fae, but one of such different powers … I stilled. Ursa was right; a person with that kind of mixed lineage would be unstoppable—depending on whose hands they ended up in.

Was that how she managed to break the bond between the queen and me? Was she somehow using her own daughter's powers?

"What does this have to do with me?"

Ursa shook her head. "I have my own games to play, little maiden, and in order for them to play out the way I want, I need allies."

"Why are you telling me all of this?"

Ursa shrugged. "I suppose it feels good to get it all out. Not like you'll be in any place to tell anyone of importance anyway."

I opened my mouth to question her when another rustle of the trees startled me. A person I never wanted to see again, not until my knife was lodged between her rib cage, appeared between two assassins.

"Queen Gemma."

I shook my head, pulling myself back to the present as realization hit me.

The queen found me.

She captured me.

No.

How did this happen? Panic surged forward, and I gasped for breath. I'd been free. The bond placed upon me had been broken, it couldn't be fixed. Then again, hadn't Ursa already lied to me?

My heart hammered against my chest as it tightened. A tingle rose from my toes and up my legs as it turned into a burning sensation. I hissed and looked at the silhouette. Why did everything hurt so badly?

"What did you do to me?"

This was more than just some hit to the head.

"Come with me," the girl beckoned, and my feet moved. I tried to stop, but they moved without me. Dread, deeper than the dread I'd felt earlier, seeped into my bones, into every piece of my soul. I knew this feeling. I may not be bound to the queen anymore, but that didn't mean I couldn't be bound to someone else.

I followed the girl out into a brightly lit hallway. With my eyes adjusted, I looked down at the girl in front of me. Curly blonde hair cascaded down her small back. Her hands placed behind her, one hand in the other as she led the way.

I guessed right. A little girl no older than ten at best. What in hells sake? Why would the queen leave me in the hands of a child?

"Wh-who are you?"

"Ah, yes, silly me. It would be wise to know your mistress's name. I'm Wendy Darling, but you can just call me Dee."

My mistress? My eyes widened. *I'm bound to a child?*

"Why am I here? Why am I bound—"

Dee whirled around. Heat flared in her cheeks as flames flickered in her light blue eyes. She gritted her teeth. "I'd choose your next words *very* carefully. I may look like one, and at times I may act like one, but don't forget I'm much older than I look, and I do not take kindly to those who underestimate me. Is that clear?"

Such words coming from such a young voice. How was I not dreaming right now? How was all of this happening?

"Crystal."

She beamed and clasped her hands together. "You've been a very bad pet, Marian. Queen Gemma wants to make sure you don't run off again. Too important, she said. So, she sent you here. To Neverland. To me. She knew I needed help with a little problem and offered you as my aid. Now enough chit chat. Time to see what all the fuss is over the queen's precious beasts."

None of this made any sense. If the queen had me in her grasp, why didn't she just kill me? I was no good to her locked away with some weird little girl. Unless I missed something.

We stopped in front of a large wooden door. Two guards on either side narrowed their eyes on me at our approach. Dee turned to me and crossed her arms over her chest.

"Shift."

Agony. Excruciating agony rippled through my body as bones popped and muscles stretched to ungodly ends. Fur sprouted along my limbs replacing my dark skin as nails extended and my ears came to a point.

Gods, let this torture end.

Yet it didn't, each second pain stabbed my skin like a thousand of the sharpest needles. Changing was never pleasant, but this, this was torture. A forced change under the magic of a witch and not the magic of the moon left the beast inside of me angry.

I wanted to die. To end my suffering once and for all, but something in the back of my mind begged me not to. A voice—a deep, rich sound that crashed over me in waves of warmth. The shift ended, and with it my agony. I panted, and my body shook with the last bit of tremors of the change.

"You're beautiful."

Dee stepped closer and scratched behind my ear. I snarled, but she didn't care. She knew I couldn't harm her. The bond ensured no damage or harm to either party. I couldn't kill her, and she couldn't kill me. I just had to do everything she said whether I wanted to or not. The idea of being in this position again, of having to bow down to a little girl ... I wanted to scream.

"I'm going to need your help here, Marian. You see, I have a little predicament that needs some attending to. A problem I can't quite crack. And now that I have you, this little egg will shatter and break and spew all of its secrets to me. You help me, and I promise to upgrade you to a much nicer room." Dee threw her head back and laughed. "Now, be a good little pup and follow me."

The door between the guards opened to another dark room. This one had a small window, enough to fit your arm through, but the moon's light filtered in enough that it wasn't in complete darkness

"Marian, I'd like you to meet a dear friend of mine. He's a bit rough around the edges, but I bet you can get him to come around."

I stilled. What did she want me to do? What could I possibly do to help her in this form?

I could have slapped myself. I was the beast. A vile creature meant to fight, meant to tear apart their opponent. Wendy needed my help, to crack an egg to reveal its secrets.

"Peter… Peter, come out and meet my new friend."

Scuffling of feet sounded from the far corner as a boy walked out into the light. Shaggy blond covered most of a dirty and sunken face. His shredded green tunic and his brown pants were just as bad. Both hung from what appeared to be skin and bones. How long had he been here?

"I won't tell you shit, Wendy. No matter what you do to me," Peter hissed. Fight still clung to him, in the way he held his ground, the way his chin lifted at his words.

His eyes flickered to me, and they widened. His mouth opened just a little as his face paled. He may not have a clue what I was, but the look in his eyes was no different than those who did. A monster, a beast worth fearing.

"You will. In time, you will." She turned to me. "Why don't you start with his pretty face? Let's show Peter why he should have given up when he had the chance, shall we?"

The pull of the demand gripped me. I yanked and tugged at my restraint, at what strength I had left. But the bond proved to be a better foe.

Peter took a step back, and then another before his back touched the wall. "Wendy, come on, don't do this. You're better than this. Please."

"You actually believe that, don't you? Poor wittle Peter, thinks he knows everything. Well, now it's my turn to know everything. And you will tell me, Peter. You will."

I stalked closer until my bared teeth were inches away from the boy's face. Tears welled in my eyes, and my heart nearly leapt from my chest as I tried to stop myself from the demand given to me.

Come on, Marian, you're better than this.

"Attack." Dee said in a calm, yet malicious tone.

The last of my strings snapped, and I lunged.

All I could hear was the cackle of Dee's laugh as my vision faded to black.

Author's Note

I sincerely hope you all enjoyed this prequel novella. It was super fun to write and definitely one of my favorites. A lot of you might be wondering why I chose to write Robin and Marian's tale instead of a prequel that fell in line with a character from book one. All I can tell you is that it will all come together as the story goes on. So, sit tight and let the author work her magic!! But, this beauty couldn't have happened without the amazing team of people behind me.

Jared, my husband, and better half who is the most amazing and supportive spouse a girl could have. Oh, and of course giving me the most beautiful boys a girl could ask for.

Rae, my best friend, and person who I look up to the most in the author world.

Nastasia, my editor who was amazing through this entire process and really helped polish this up to being one of my favorite stories to date!

If you enjoyed this retelling, you could also check out another retelling I did in an anthology called Fractured Folklore. The story I wrote is a Snow White retelling titled The Deadliest Snow. This story will be getting revamped at some point to incorporate a new (Urban Fantasy) series I'll be writing in the future.

If you like the Urban Fantasy setting you can also check out my short story in Blood and Betrayal titled Cursed in Blood.

Like what you've read and want to keep tabs on what's to come? You can follow me on Instagram or Facebook, you can join my Facebook group Jay R. Wolf's Pack, or you can also sign up for my newsletter!

About the Author

Jay R. Wolf is an author of dark and urban fantasy, a wife and mother, and a huge geek.

She is from a small town in Michigan and moved to the big city to pursue her dream of acing. Though her dream of racing cars is in the wind, she finds herself in a comfy lifestyle in the Mile High city where writing fantasy has become a passion.

Her other hobbies include long walks in ancient forests where the wild things roam, gaming against evil foes, and catching fish in the great lakes.

Want to know more?
Website: www.authorjayrwolf.com
Facebook/Instagram @authorjayrwolf